THE
Wendy Puzzle

THE
Wendy Puzzle

Florence Parry Heide

Holiday House / New York

Library of Congress Cataloging in Publication Data

Heide, Florence Parry.
The Wendy puzzle.

SUMMARY: When high school senior Wendy alienates all
her friends, her sister finds the reason for Wendy's
puzzling behavior in her secret love poems.
I. Title.
PZ7.H36We   [Fic]   82-80818
ISBN 0-8234-0463-3   AACR2

This is for you, Judy Girl,
with much love to you and Kim
from Mom

THE
Wendy Puzzle

Chapter 1

"Tell me a story, Dodie."

My kid sister, Cissy, and I were alone in the house for a change. This was my favorite kind of Saturday, my favorite kind of time, just Cissy and me. No problems, no pressures, no aggravations, no confrontations, no Wendy. Just being.

Mom was over at Feebee's Fountain of Beauty having a permanent. Dad was playing golf with Uncle Frank. And Wendy, my older sister, was off terrorizing someone somewhere. I knew she was because she always was yelling angrily about something or nothing, making a scene, acting like and looking like an old witch. That's what the kids at her high school were calling her: Wendy the Witch.

Every conversation with her turned into an argument, then a quarrel, then a real scene. So if you were smart you kept your mouth shut when you were around her. If the government could harness all that energy there wouldn't be an energy crisis. But then they'd have Wendy, and that would be worse.

"Tell me a story, Dodie."

"In a minute, Cissy. I promised Dad I'd get this batch of pictures in the album."

"Okay." Cissy carried her dolls and toys over to the couch and continued her singsong never-ending games with them. Everything about Cissy is soft and easy, quiet and nice. Nice. The way Wendy used to be. I wondered for the millionth time when it was and why it was that Wendy had changed from sweet to sour.

I had two easy jobs this afternoon. One, taking care of Cissy. Two, putting into a new album all of the last family snapshots. Snapshots! Dad would never forgive me for calling them that. Photographs: that's better. He calls himself a photography buff but he's a photography *nut*. He practically lives in the darkroom he's built in the basement. Maybe he went down there to escape from Wendy. Now that I thought about it, the darkroom was the only safe place in the house.

I was sitting at a card table in the living room, and I'd spread out all the snapshots—photographs—so I could put them in order.

I'd put off this job for so long that there were about a hundred pictures now, and Dad had been nagging me all week to do it. I'd have finished this project ages ago if he'd been willing to get one of those Eze-Do albums, where all you have to do is stick a sheet of plastic over the pictures, but oh, no. That wasn't good enough because this album was going to be a permanent record of the family. An *heirloom*.

So the album had to be real leather, and the pictures had to be glued in so they'd never fall out, even in a million years.

I sorted them so they were in chronological order, and then I spread them out on the floor so I'd have room for the album on the card table. This was spring, and the first ones had been taken late last summer.

Had we changed?

Mom and Dad looked just about the same now as they had then, except for Mom's new hairdo and Dad's old mustache, which he finally shaved off.

I looked at the pictures of me: I was sure a lot taller now: wow. Maybe I'd grow up to be a giant. And my nose was longer now. Probably from blowing it so much. I felt as if I'd been born with this cold. And the shoes I was wearing last summer were about ten pairs of shoes ago. I have to get new shoes practically every week.

But it was still the same me, still the same person, the same personality, the same Dodie Moffitt.

Cissy had grown up a lot, I realized. I hadn't noticed, day by day. Now I looked quickly over at her, afraid for a minute that I'd see her changing right before my eyes into a grown kid.

She was still the same Cissy, just as I was still the same Dodie; just older. She has a tiny eager face, baby-sized like her nose and mouth; her eyes are pretty small, too, but you don't have to have great big eyes to see. Her bangs were getting too long—Mom would probably cut them tonight. For real haircuts, she takes Cissy to Fee-bee's. There is something sweet and bittersweet about four years old. I didn't want Cissy to grow up.

Buggsy was lying beside me, and I started rubbing his head, just behind the ears where he really likes it.

"Hey, Buggsy," I said. "When did you stop being a kitten and start being a cat? What day was it?"

Buggsy stretched, got to his feet, and stalked away. He hates philosophical questions.

I looked back at the pictures. The one who had really changed, really *changed*, was Wendy.

In the pictures of last summer, Wendy still looked like the old Wendy, her head tilted sideways, smiling into the camera, her eyes kind, her hair soft, and her face easy, happy. Now, with her hair skinned back tight, her chin jutting forward, her eyes narrowed and angry, her mouth thin and down-turning, her shoulders hunched, she looked like a mean old spiteful woman.

I'd seen these pictures before, so there were no surprises. But now I started to look for the shift from the Wendy I remembered to Wendy the Witch. Was there any special day that it happened? Was it something on the outside that made it happen, or something on the inside? Maybe she'd been born with a tiny little seed of mean in her, and the seed had just sprouted and grown.

I put the pictures in the big album, fastening them securely and forever in place for Cissy's and my great-grandchildren to admire. Wendy wouldn't have any great-grandchildren because no one would ever want to marry her. "And this was your Great Aunt Gwendolyn. They called her Wendy, Wendy the Witch of Weird."

I leafed through the big album once again. It was like seeing those nature programs on TV with those time-lapse photography tricks: from seed to bud to flower to wilt right before your eyes—from Wendy to Witchhood.

The phone rang, and I answered it. I love to be the one to answer, even if everyone is home. There's always the outside chance that it will be something surprising, something wonderful.

"Miss Dorothy Moffitt, please."

A voice I couldn't recognize.

"This is Dorothy Moffitt."

"Miss Moffitt, your name has been selected as the winner in the sixty-thousand-dollar sweepstakes. Your check is being forwarded today."

It was Jill, disguising her voice. "Don't you have anything better to do than make obscene phone calls?" I asked.

"Nope. What are you up to?"

"Nothing. I'm sitting with Cissy. Want to come over?"

"Nope. I just washed my hair."

I reached up and felt mine. Grease city! I'd wash it tonight for sure. "Come over wet."

"Can't. Have to study."

"Oh." I never studied, not if I could help it. Jill was brighter than I was, but she didn't *act* bright. We never talked about school. She was in accelerated classes, and I wasn't. Maybe if we hadn't known each other since we were five we wouldn't have been friends. Maybe she'd have just had friends who were A students.

"I just wanted to check up on you, make sure you weren't doing anything naughty, disgusting, or illegal. Call you tonight, okay?"

"Okay, 'by." We'd probably talk six more times today.

"Let's play Bad Guys, Dodie."

"Okay, Cissy."

Bad Guys: it was one of Cissy's favorite games. "The Bad Guys are after us, the Bad Guys are after us!" I liked it as much as Cissy: I'd make a good mother. Or else I was slightly retarded.

Cissy and I sat in the big rocking chair and rocked faster and faster.

The Bad Guys were sometimes pirates, sometimes wild fierce animals, or monsters, or creatures from outer space. We rocked faster and faster to escape. The rocking chair was a ship or an airplane, a raft or maybe a train. Today it was a flying carpet, and huge ugly birds were chasing us through clouds and rainbows.

"Faster, faster," Cissy cried happily. "Hurry, they'll catch us!" Of course Cissy and I always won. That's the advantage of making up your own rules.

The back door slammed, so hard that I knew it was Wendy. Another slam: Wendy's library books thrown on the kitchen table.

"Faster, faster!" said Cissy.

I have news for you, I wanted to say. We can beat the big birds, or the pirates, but we can't escape from Wendy. She'll eat us alive: hold tight.

Sure enough. "All these lights! Can't you get it through your head that you've got to turn off the lights when you don't need them? It's a waste, a terrible waste of energy!"

I heard the refrigerator door being opened, then a smothered angry exclamation. Another slam. Cissy dropped her voice to a whisper. "Faster, Dodie!"

I knew Wendy would ruin our game, ruin our time.

"What's that junk doing in the refrigerator?" she demanded, striding into the living room.

I knew what she meant: the Marshomelts I'd bought at Bruno's. I'd meant to hide them at the back of the refrigerator. I kept rocking with Cissy, trying not to pay attention. "Treats for dessert," I said. I should have ignored her, but you couldn't win, no matter what you did.

"How many times do I have to tell this stupid family that stuff like that is pure trash?"

9

"I don't know, maybe a million times," I said.

"You know there's no nourishment in that junk, just fluff and poison. Poison!"

"Look," I said crossly, "one lousy laboratory rat eats six million Marshomelts and gets sick. So now one little bite of one little Marshomelt is going to give the whole world cancer."

Cissy climbed down from the rocking chair and walked over to her dolls on the couch. Our game of Bad Guys was spoiled.

"Don't you ever read anything?" Wendy demanded.

"Not if I can help it," I said. "If reading all that stuff is what makes you so disagreeable, I'm afraid to read. Talk about poisoning your system!"

She ignored me.

"You should be protecting Cissy, not encouraging her to eat that junk you drag into this house. She's too little to know the difference, but you're not. You're irresponsible!"

Why did we always end up having a pitched battle? Now my heart was beating fast, and I felt rotten. And suddenly more than anything in the world I wanted some jelly beans. Not one, but a whole packet. Maybe a hundred packets. Arguing with Wendy always had this effect on me. It was her fault that I had become a jelly bean freak. I'd hidden some, in their nonbiodegradable plastic packets, up on the top shelf in the kitchen, behind the plates we never use. I knew there were three packets left.

10

I should have taken them down before Wendy came back. Now it was too late. I'd have to find a better hiding place. Not in our room—she'd ferret them out. Wendy has a sixth sense about junk food.

Wendy kept raving: about the Marshomelts, about cancer-producing sugar substitutes, about wasting water and electricity and coal and oil and everything else. You'd think I was in charge of destroying the planet and everything on it. I kept thinking about how I absolutely positively had to get those jelly beans, and Cissy kept trying to talk softly to her dolls in an effort to drown out Wendy's voice.

"If anything's making anybody sick, it's you with all this hassling all the time," I said crossly. "Come on, Cissy, let's get our shoes on and go for a walk, okay?"

"How can you all be so stupid? Stupid, stupid, stupid!" yelled Wendy, storming upstairs and slamming the door to our room.

I could probably risk climbing up now for the jelly beans, as long as she was safely upstairs, but I wanted to get out of the house anyway. It wasn't big enough to hold anyone but Wendy: just knowing she was there filled up all the corners, all the empty spaces, with white heat.

I walked with Cissy to Bruno's: I'd get some jelly beans there. I needed a change of scene, and I needed to walk off all this extra adrenaline that had swooshed through my system when Wendy had appeared on the horizon.

Bruno's Palace was only a few blocks away. Everything in the town is close to everything else, so I could walk almost anywhere. The Palace didn't look like much: one counter, two wooden tables with red plastic covers and chairs to match, three very sick-looking plants. A cash register, old-fashioned, maybe a million years old. A cuckoo clock, wildly and hideously beautiful. It cuckooed every fifteen minutes. Much ado about nothing: like Wendy, jumping out to say Boo. The world was going to go on in spite of Wendy's alarms.

In the big window wall facing the street was a cardboard sign that said OPEN on one side and (guess what) CLOSED on the other. When you were inside looking out, it looked as if the sign meant that the outside was closed.

A couple of shelves in a glass display case held, among other things, jelly beans in nonbiodegradable plastic packets. And behind the counter was a shelf displaying Bruno's super homemade pies, for which he was famous. Truck drivers were always stopping in just for the special pie of the day. Some of the drivers were local and came in about every day, and some were long distance and came only once every week or two. Truck drivers and kids from school were Bruno's best customers.

Bruno was reading the newspaper at one of the tables. "Enter the Moffitt sisters," he announced as we walked in.

"Two of them, anyway," I said.

"I've already had my daily encounter with the third," he said, smiling ruefully. His face creased into even more wrinkles, lines, and furrows.

"She stopped in earlier to give me a hard time about the cigarette machine and the candy bars and pop and gum. If I don't get rid of all the junk, she's going to organize a picket line."

"I guess some people are just born picketers," I said, eyeing the jelly beans.

Bruno stretched and pushed his paper aside. "So what can I do for you, young ladies?" he asked. "Conversation, checkers, stories or other fancies, or a piece of blueberry pie, hot from the oven?"

I'd really just come in for the jelly beans, but now all of a sudden I also had a craving for blueberry pie, my favorite.

"Four packets of jelly beans plus a super gigantic piece of pie," I decided. "You'll have some pie, too, won't you, Cissy?"

She nodded and climbed up on one of the stools.

"It's sure restful having customers like you two," said Bruno, lifting the pie down from the shelf and setting it on the counter. "I don't know if I'd have the strength to stay in business if all my customers shouted at me like your noble sister Wendy. She makes me feel guilty, and I'm not a bad guy."

"Don't listen," I advised him.

"Impossible," he said. "Here's your pie. Blueberry blue, huckleberry berries."

Cissy and I joined him in the chant:

H, U, uckle

B, U, uckle

H, U, uckle I

H, U, uckle

B, U, uckle

Huckleberry pie!

A Foodster truck pulled up in the driveway, and I looked through the big window to see Jobe, Bruno's nephew, jumping out on the passenger side. Good: I was hoping I'd see him today. Jobe was another reason I liked Bruno's. He unloaded a big box from the truck and brought it in. It must have been pretty lightweight because he balanced it on his head and made juggling motions with his arms. I knew he must have seen Cissy and me and was doing it for our benefit.

"Greetings, salutations, and hello," he said as he pushed the door open. "Having a jelly bean sandwich, Dodie?" Jobe was the tallest and thinnest guy I knew. And the nicest.

He set the box down. "Potato chips, Cornlets, Softuns, and Puffballs," he announced. "Enough junk food to keep us in business all week."

He shook his head, and his limp hair flopped in his eyes. He tossed it back and ran his fingers through it. No

14

wonder his hair is so limp, I thought. It's exhausted from so much activity.

The driver came in with another box.

"Hey, Bucky," said Bruno. "It's blue, blue, blueberry pie today."

"Terrific," said Bucky, setting the box down. "Coffee with the pie, cream with the coffee, conversation with the cream, cards with the conversation," he said, walking over to one of the tables. I'd seen Bucky several times before. He had bright red hair and a bright pink round face and always wore a baseball cap with a huge visor. He pushed his cap back and winked at me.

For Bruno, every customer was a friend. Now he sat at the table with this one. Bruno's wife, Jess, had died a year ago. Jobe was his nephew. He came for the funeral on his way to college and then he just stayed on, helping Bruno, and he moved into the apartment over the Palace where Bruno and Jess had lived.

Bruno kept telling him to get going, get off to college, and Jobe kept postponing it. "No sense in going to college until I've made up my mind what I want to study, right? Don't want to learn one single thing that I don't have to."

I'd listen to lots of their talks about it while I was sitting at the counter eating pie or having a Coke or buying jelly beans.

"You're not learning a thing around here," I'd heard Bruno say last week. "Not a blessed thing."

"You'd be surprised. Besides, college isn't everything, it isn't necessarily the end of the rainbow. I'm deciding which direction I want to go. I'm learning lots of things."

"What kinds of things?" Bruno had asked, and Jobe had shrugged and smiled that terrific smile of his. "I guess I really like this funny little town. Right now Wellsburg, Illinois, suits me. Far from city life, city noise, city people, city stuff and nonsense. It suits me, for now. Not forever, maybe, but now. Maybe not tomorrow, but today."

I finished my pie, and then I finished Cissy's. Jobe was filling the display case with the stuff the Foodster truck had brought, and Cissy was helping. Bruno was still playing cards with Bucky.

"You may be a good piemaker, Bruno, but you're a rotten cardplayer," said Bucky.

"I'm a fine cardplayer. It's just that I let you win once in a while. It's good for your ego."

I put my money down on the counter and picked up the packets of jelly beans.

"Here's a paper bag," said Jobe. "You don't want those jelly bean packets sliding all over. And you don't want Eagle Eye to see them, either. She might bomb the place if she thought we were still selling you jelly beans, and I'm too young to die."

His hair fell over his eyes again, and he brushed it away. He smiled at me. With a smile like that, he

16

wouldn't have to go to college. He could get to be President.

"How do you manage to get by the dragon at the gate, Dodie? How do you sneak those wicked teeth-rotting chewables past your ferocious sister, anyway? Aren't you afraid she'll find out and—" He drew his finger across his throat dramatically.

"What I buy with my own money is my own business. And what I eat is my own business," I lied. "I don't try to tell her what to do. She doesn't have to tell me."

"Ah, but she does."

"I know. But I don't have to listen."

"Yes, you do. She'll just talk louder and harder and longer."

"It's just a phase," I told him.

"Maybe," he said. "And maybe if you stay at one stage too long that's the way you'll turn out to be forever and ever."

He pulled at his lip. Keep smiling, I wanted to say.

"She takes things too hard, that's all," he said. "Things bother her. Things make her angry."

"I'm too dumb to care about all that stuff," I said.

"You're just not interested. Wendy cares so much it hurts." He scratched his ear. "You're soft and easy. Wendy's all sharp corners, but she's a very stimulating person."

Stimulating! No one could ever accuse me of that.

17

I put the jelly beans in the paper bag. Jobe finished emptying the Foodster boxes. "Hey, your mom said she wanted me to save her some empty boxes. Maybe I'll bring these over there sometime, okay? Save her a trip."

"Sure," I said. "Any time. Just remember that if Wendy sees you with empty junk-food boxes, she'll have an excuse to yell at you and the rest of the world. Not that she ever needs an excuse to yell."

"I'll yell back."

"That will be the day. You don't know how to yell. You don't even know how to frown convincingly."

"I'll have to start practicing, I guess."

The cuckoo clock started chiming the hour. "Three!" shouted Cissy happily.

"Your teeth are blue," said Jobe. "So are yours," he added, looking at my mouth. "You'd better keep your lips sealed when you get home or you'll be in real trouble."

He smiled again. Honestly, if he could patent his smile he'd be a millionaire.

Chapter 2

When I opened the back door I couldn't tell whether Wendy was home or not. Was she upstairs in our room, getting ready for another attack on the family or on the school or on some unsuspecting passerby? Or had she gone off somewhere to picket or demonstrate or argue?

I listened. Silence. I didn't want to go upstairs and check in case she was up there in our room. I hid two packets of jelly beans and divided the rest with Cissy. I hated sharing a room with Wendy, but there were only three bedrooms and Cissy's room was too small for more than one bed. I could hardly wait until next year when Wendy would be going off to college. I'd have my own room and my own peace of mind. Everything would be cheerful and easy.

I called Jill. "If you can say Saskatchewan backwards I'll give you all my jelly beans."

"The word you are searching for is Wanbawee," she said.

"Close," I told her, and hung up.

Cissy had arranged her jelly beans according to colors, the way she always did, and then ate one from each little pile. "A black one, a pink one, a white one, a green one." I always saved black ones until last; they were my favorites.

"Tell me a story, Dodie."

"Okay. What about?"

"About Buggsy." She sat on the couch with her dolls, Lolamay Parsley and Quimby Lee. Buggsy rubbed against my legs, purring, and I picked him up and sat down next to Cissy.

"Okay. Once upon a time, long before there were airplanes or cars—"

"Or chairs," said Cissy.

"Or anything. Long, long ago, once upon a time, cats had no names. No separate names. They were all called cats. Cat number three, cat number ten, and so on."

Buggsy jumped off my lap. He didn't like stories.

"That was all right for a while, but then of course there got to be more and more cats. So then the cats were called cat number three thousand and ten and so on."

"And a billion million," said Cissy.

"Yes. And they began to run out of numbers. So they had to start making up names. And that's why Buggsy is

Buggsy instead of cat number six thousand million and three."

The back door slammed. Mom must be home. Or was it Wendy? I stiffened.

"Hi ho!"

It was Mom. I relaxed.

Cissy ran out to the kitchen, and I followed her.

"Hey, Mom, I like your hair." I did. It looked terrific, she looked terrific. She looked a lot younger than Wendy, for sure.

"Thanks. I keep trying to beat middle age. No one ever has, but everyone has to give it a try anyway."

"Maybe you'll be the first one in history to win."

She shook her head.

"It's rigged, like the Bad Guy game. Knowing how it's going to turn out is part of the fun. Well, not part of the *fun* actually, part of the game."

She looked at the kitchen clock. "Want to help me pull supper together?"

"Sure."

"We can eat early. I promised Annie I'd help her sew nursery curtains tonight."

Annie—I call her AnnTanny—is Mom's kid sister. When I was little, I always thought Dad and Mom were saying AnnTanny instead of Aunt Annie. AnnTanny and Frank lived just a couple of blocks from us. Their first baby was due this fall. Since AnnTanny had had two

21

miscarriages and nearly another one this last time, she was really careful. I mean, really *careful.* She didn't do a thing. Not even marketing. Uncle Frank and Mom did everything for her. AnnTanny had never been strong like Mom and these days she acted really weak and helpless. And she was so afraid she'd get a cold or something that now that I had my long spring cold, she wouldn't even let me come over. Silly.

"Can you fix the carrots, Dodie?"

I always liked these times, poking around in the kitchen with Mom, Cissy sitting at the kitchen table, coloring. This was the way our life should be: no fuss, no Wendy.

"Mom, when did Wendy start being a witch?"

"Oh, Dodie." Mom hates philosophical questions as much as Buggsy does.

"Well, when did she?" I asked again, scraping the carrots. "Because she wasn't always like this. She used to be nice. What started all this meanness?"

Mom sighed. Talking about Wendy always made her sigh, and no wonder. It must be terrible to see your own daughter turn into a freak.

"I just don't know," said Mom. "Maybe it's just growing pains."

I'd scraped the carrots and now I started to grind the peelings up in the garbage disposal. I caught Mom glancing from it to the back door nervously. Of course. She was afraid Wendy would come in and find us using the

22

disposal. We'd be in for another big scene. I remembered that first time with it a couple of months ago. Dad had bought the thing, the first we'd ever had. We'd been cleaning up after supper. In our family everyone has a job and we rotate them: clearer, scraper, loader, sweeper, and so on.

Well, I'd been scraping the throwaways into the disposal and suddenly Wendy had walked in. She'd reached over and turned it off. "Stop using that. It's horrible," she said. "All that food going down, all mixed up with soap and junk. It's wasted, all wasted. It should be used. That's nature's way, it's all part of the cycle. This way, it's no good to anything, not to animals, not to the earth."

"Let's keep moving," said Dad. "I've got some prints in the dryer that I want to get back to."

Wendy had straightened and turned around to face Dad. "Food that isn't eaten should be returned to the earth, not all ground up with soapsuds. And where is it all going? To pollute this world instead of feeding and nourishing it, the way it's supposed to."

Dad had spoken calmly. "Well, sweetie, we've got this machine now, we're going to use it. It won't spoil the whole world."

Wendy looked at Dad scornfully. Then she turned to Mom. "Mom, you can't use this thing. Rip it out. Or at least unplug it."

"Well, dear, I think we have to be reasonable," said Mom.

"I'm the one who's being reasonable," shouted Wendy.

"Now, honey," Dad said, trying to smooth her down, "one garbage disposal more or less isn't going to change anything. I've bought it, I've paid for it, and we'll hear no more about it. After all, it's only one unit and there are thousands and thousands."

"So one more won't make any difference, is that it?" Wendy demanded shrilly. "Everyone's doing it, so why can't we? That isn't good enough for me. It shouldn't be good enough for you!"

Dad's voice had risen. "Wait a minute, young lady. We don't need any hassle. Let's get this kitchen cleaned up so we can all get back to more important business."

"There's no more important business than the world we live in!" Wendy had shouted, running out of the kitchen, and when she slammed the door to our room upstairs, the house shook.

Now I ground up the rest of the carrot peelings. Surprise, surprise: I finished with the disposal and still no Wendy. One scene avoided, only sixty million to go, probably.

"Maybe she's at the library again," said Mom hopefully. "She's been working so hard on that research for the debate. She's probably just overtired." Mom's face brightened. "That's it, she's just overtired. It's that work and worry about the debate. I'll be glad when it's over."

Poor Mom. She'd always keep thinking up new excuses

24

for Wendy's being so lousy and mean. I was sure the upcoming debate had nothing to do with anything. But if thinking that it did cheered Mom up, that was fine.

Mom started to make some kind of sauce for the chicken. I'd have plenty of time before supper to wash my limp and lumpy hair. Besides, taking a long shower always relaxed me. Standing under the spray calmed my nerves and improved my brain. I'd been taking more and more showers lately because of Wendy.

I called Jill. "Don't call me for an hour. I'm washing my brain."

"Don't let it shrink," said Jill.

"Shrink, shrank, shrunk. It's pea-sized to begin with," I told her.

"Stop bragging," she said, and hung up.

I thought about the debate while I was standing under the shower washing my hair: suds and rinse, suds and rinse, a zillion times. Maybe that would get the lumps and sags and knots and wilts out. Out of my hair, and out of my brain.

It was true that Wendy had been doing a lot of research, getting ready for the debate—maybe she *was* just overtired. (See, the shower was calming me down already, making me kinder.)

I wouldn't care how much I had to study if I could be studying with someone like Saul Hogan, who was Wendy's partner in this whole debate thing. He had to be the nicest guy in the whole senior class. Wendy, with her nose in her books and papers, probably hadn't even noticed his eyes, which were spectacularly mind-boggling.

This was the way the debate program worked at the high school. In January everyone in debate, which meant any senior who was really interested and involved and had certain grades, like all A's and B's, drew lots for a general subject. Things like abortion, euthanasia, death penalty, and so on. The other senior who drew the same subject as you, became your debate partner.

You both researched your subject, working together, reading everything you could about it, finding out all kinds of facts and figures and statistics, and learning what leading specialists on both sides of the question thought about it.

After you finished the research, working together and helping each other, you drew straws to see which side you were going to debate on: for or against, good or bad, pro or con, affirmative or negative, yes or no.

Saul Hogan and Wendy had drawn nuclear power. They'd both been studying everything about it ever since. Usually they'd meet at the library and work there; sometimes on Sundays Saul Hogan would come over to our house and they'd work at the dining room table. I never saw Wendy look at his eyes, not a single time. What a waste.

Once in a while he'd find an article on his own, and

then he'd copy it for Wendy. Sometimes she'd find one and copy it for him. This had gone on for three or four months now, and soon they'd be finding out which side each of them was going to have to debate on. The debate was scheduled for the first of May.

The teacher in charge of the debate thing was Dr. Ellis Somers. Doctor! He was the only one with a doctorate in the whole high school, everyone else was Mr. or Ms. This was his first year in Wellsburg. I'd never met him but his picture had been in the paper when he first came to town: horn-rimmed glasses and a stern look, sort of like a humanoid owl. Wendy really liked him—as much as she could like anybody. I heard her tell Saul Hogan one night that she had one of Dr. Somers' little notebooks and was memorizing it. "He has goofy handwriting, but nobody's perfect. He's got some great ideas." She'd picked up the notebook and leafed through it quickly. "He was going to throw this away, so I just took it. I know practically every word. Listen to this, for instance: . . ." And she was off again, with never a thought about Saul or his eyes. It was all about the power of ideas, and how ideas can actually be a physical force, or something boring like that.

As I stood under the shower I thought once more about Saul Hogan and those astonishing eyes. It wasn't just the color, bluish green, or maybe greenish blue, or the size (enormous), or the position (far apart), but some kind of extra light in them or something. I could never figure it out, but of course I didn't see him all that much. If I'd been Wendy, seeing him every day at school and most afternoons after school and some evenings and Sundays, I'd have been able to decide what it was that gave his eyes all that extra glow. It was all wasted on Wendy, who didn't even know he *had* eyes.

I sighed, and sudsed and rinsed one more time. Why couldn't I have had irresistible eyes? Why couldn't I have had hair that bounced? Why couldn't I have had feet that grew just so far and no farther? Why couldn't I have been just a straight-A whiz kid instead of a mediocre C sort of person? Why couldn't . . . . I always counted and recounted all of my failings under the shower so that I could maybe stop thinking about them other times.

Suds, rinse, suds, rinse.

Bang! Bang! Bang!

It was Wendy pounding on the bathroom door. "Get out of that shower! You're using enough water for fifty people! Haven't you heard there's a water shortage?"

I pretended I hadn't heard. But she'd ruined my shower. And my mood. And my day. As always.

Maybe I could get some earplugs so I wouldn't hear her. And a blindfold so I wouldn't have to see her, either.

I stayed in the bathroom as long as I possibly could and then opened the door cautiously. Maybe Wendy would go berserk some day, maybe today, and maybe we'd all make headlines:

MADDENED SISTER KILLS FAMILY, MARS WEEKEND.

She was sitting at the desk, hunched over, reading. She didn't even look up. I was saved. For the moment.

By the time I'd come downstairs, hair still wet, Dad was back from his golf game with Uncle Frank and was playing cards at the card table with Cissy, his own version of Old Maid. Mom was sitting at the kitchen desk writing a letter. She loved to do that, this time of day: very restful. And that way, as she often explained, she could be sure nothing burned or dried up or boiled away or boiled over or stuck together. She had a huge pad of paper, every sheet a different pastel color. Wendy and I each had one, too, Christmas presents from AnnTanny and Uncle Frank.

"Hi, babe," said Dad. "I'm afraid Cissy's going to win this game. I don't know how she does it, but she does." He looked the way he always did after an afternoon of golf or fishing: rosy, relaxed, and handsome. Of course, he and Uncle Frank didn't fish much anymore; the fish that were in our local lake and river had died or were sickly. I'd never got over my yen to sit in his lap, but of course I was too old for lap sitting now, just as I was too old for tears and dolls and little feet and Old Maid and the Bad Guy game.

"I put the pictures in," I said before he could ask me.

"Terrific. Let me look. Cissy, you beat me again.

Would you put the cards away?" I went to get the album. Dad had had it lettered: VOLUME FIVE—SPRINGS AND SUMMERS OF GWENDOLYN, DOROTHY, AND CYNTHIA.

I put it on the card table. Dad admired it, turning the pages slowly, commenting at each turn: "You did a great job, Dodie. Now we're all caught up except for the pictures I'm printing this weekend. We'll have to start a new album. I wonder what the pictures in that one will be?"

He stood up, walked over to the big comfy rocker, and sat down. "I'm so relaxed, I'm practically asleep," he said. "I feel like a cooked noodle."

Cissy climbed up on his lap. I knew Dad would have liked it just as much as I would have if I'd been little again, like Cissy, sitting in his lap, rocking, maybe playing Bad Guys one more time. What would he do when Cissy grew up? Well, he'd have AnnTanny and Uncle Frank's little kid. But that wouldn't be the same. It would be like borrowing a kid instead of having your own built-in one.

"I'm happy to announce that I haven't had a constructive thought all day," said Dad contentedly.

"That's what weekends are for," I told him. That's what they should be for, anyway, I thought. Probably Wendy didn't even know it was Saturday. She was too busy thinking about the problems of the universe. Every day was a Wendy day for her.

"This is all I can think about now, for instance," Dad went on. "I'm thinking that tonight's dinner smells very enticing indeed. And I'm wondering how Mom makes chicken taste like something else altogether."

"She adds mysterious things," I said. "Maybe she could write a cookbook."

"And we'd all be rich," said Dad, rocking Cissy, whose thumb was now in her mouth. And she'd been almost over the thumb sucking routine. Maybe if I was in Dad's lap, rocking, I'd start sucking my thumb again, too. Baby habits die hard.

"All we need is a good title for the cookbook," I said.

Dad considered. "How to make something you're tired of taste like something else."

"That's it," I told him. "*The Something Else Cookbook.* Now we have the idea, and the title. All Mom has to do is write the book."

"We'll talk her into it at supper," Dad decided.

Wendy will probably ruin it all, the way she always ruins everything, I wanted to say, but I kept my thoughts to myself. Dad's mood was too happy for me to be the one to spoil it.

Mom came in from the kitchen. "There. I've written three letters and feel virtuous," she said. "And nothing boiled over or dried up. Want to see what I'm taking over to Annie's tonight?"

Mom took a present over to AnnTanny and her baby-to-be almost every time she went there, and that was every day. Well, that's what I'd do, years from now, if Cissy were pregnant and living in the next block. I never think of Wendy that way: thing one, she'd never get married and have a baby; thing two, she'd never stay in Wellsburg; thing three, I'd be the last person in the world she'd want to see. All I wanted in life was to stay right in the same town with the same people, marry someone like Dad—or Jobe. Jobe? I'd never even thought of that before, and I surprised myself by blushing. And have a family. And a life just like Mom's. Only without a Wendy. No hassle. Just plain vanilla, easy. Easy. Not even any school, or exams, or classes, or papers, or history teachers, or *any*thing. No arguments. That part would be easy without a Wendy.

Mom took a present out of the closet, wrapped in baby paper and with two big balloons attached to it. One pink, one blue. "A blue nightgown inside the package, and a pink," she said.

"Twins?" asked Dad, raising his eyebrows.

"How I wish," sighed Mom. "I just had to have one of each so Annie wouldn't think I was partial to one or the other."

"Come on, now, admit it," said Dad, smiling. "You hope she'll have a girl so you can get rid of all those little girl clothes you've been hoarding."

"I've already promised them to Cissy for her dolls." Mom sat on the arm of the rocking chair and ruffled Cissy's hair.

I wished I had a picture of that scene for the next album: Mom with her terrific new hairdo and her beautiful all-time face; Dad relaxed and smiling; Cissy, the perfect little person, covered with loving kindness and only minimal traces of this afternoon's blueberry pie. Well, at least I had a mental picture of them all; maybe that's the best kind, anyway.

It didn't last. The scene didn't change but the faces did, the heartbeats did: from smooth to sharp, from ease to hard, in a flash.

It started the second the door to our room slammed: hard, of course. Wendy was about to arrive on the scene, and we all fastened our mental seatbelts. Slam, bang, bangity bang: Wendy was coming downstairs. "The McCabes are spraying again," she said. "I'm going over to get them to stop."

"Wendy, they aren't doing anything against the law. If Bob McCabe wants to spray his trees or his bushes or his throat, it's his business, not mine, and not yours. Don't go over there making another scene."

Wendy thrust her head forward. "What people do to the air and to the world is everyone's business. Do you know what's in that pesticide of his? Do you know the damage it does?" She ran through the kitchen and slammed the back door. Poor Mr. McCabe. He couldn't call his yard his own, not with Wendy as a next door neighbor. Maybe he'd have to move away to get rid of her.

Dad sighed. I knew he was thinking the same thing I was: Wendy has got to go. One more month, and we wouldn't have a friend left.

Mom shook her head worriedly. "Janice McCabe told me that Bob was getting very upset about Wendy's coming over to yell at him all the time. They can't even sit outside and enjoy their own yard this spring, because of Wendy and her scenes. That's a fine situation."

"Well, we can't muzzle her," said Dad.

"Now that's an idea," I said.

The phone rang, and I answered it. It was for Wendy: Clay Priestly, from school. He often called about assignments. I told him she'd call back. I couldn't imagine why anyone would want to call Wendy about anything. Ever. I could hear her shrill voice even from inside. Poor Mr. McCabe.

I called Jill. "The Surgeon General has determined that telephone calls may be hazardous to your health. Unplug, disconnect, and dispose of all units as soon as possible. This announcement is brought to you by the courtesy of Illinois Bell."

"How did your hair turn out?" asked Jill.

"Wet," I told her, and hung up.

Dad had started to tell Mom about the cookbook. "You do all the work and I'll be business manager," he said.

"And I'll be the chief taster," I said.

"The Something Else Cookbook," mused Mom. "We could call tonight's supper the Great Chicken Wonder. And the salad, composed entirely of leftovers surrounded by lettuce, could be—"

That's as far as our discussion got: Wendy stormed in again, bringing in all her anger, taking up all the room.

"Stupid man! 'It's my yard, Wendy,' " she mimicked. "I told him it might be his yard but it wasn't his air. Besides, you can't really own your own land, not really *own* it. It's just entrusted to you. And he's shooting poison into everything over there. 'It's just bugs, Wendy, and the bugs are eating my trees.' " She made a face. "He can't get it through his thick head that you kill the good bugs along with the destructive ones. And the birds eat the bugs with the poison in them, and then—"

"Calm down, sweetie," Dad interrupted. "It's not worth getting excited about."

"Not worth getting excited about?" echoed Wendy angrily. "And just what *is* worth getting excited about, may I ask? The plague? An atomic bomb? The end of the world?"

I tried to sidetrack her. "That guy from school called. Clay Priestly. I said you'd call him back right away. It's important. It's about some rally, I think."

I'd added that last part about the rally because I thought it might get her mind off Mr. McCabe. Things like rallies, demonstrations, letters to editors, senators, congressmen, the President of the United States, were always sure to get her interested and involved. And usually out of the house. For all I knew, Clay Priestly had called her about some assignment; no boy could possibly call Wendy about a *date*. You'd have to be crazy, or a masochist, or a crazy masochist.

At least it got her out of our hair for a few minutes.

She'd gone upstairs to use the hall phone. For a change, I couldn't hear her shrill angry voice. She seemed to be talking like a regular person in quiet sentences, none of which I could decipher. Maybe it was a math or history assignment he'd called about. In a couple of minutes, still talking, she carried the phone into our room and shut the door.

Nobody ever called *me.* Certainly never about a *date*— I'd never had one. Come to think about it, Jill was the only person who ever called me about anything.

Jill Spooner was my best friend. We'd always been best friends. We'd played dolls and built clubhouses and had lemonade stands and shared a pet rabbit one summer and a million secrets all our lives. She'd never had a date, either. Well, we were too young. Nobody in this town ever dated anyone until they were in high school. It would be different, in a city. And it would be different if I were five feet five, had little dainty feet, shining hair, and a turned-up nose.

By the time I was old enough to have a date, a real date, my feet would be six miles long. And I'd be taller than any man or boy ever born.

Chapter 3

It hadn't been about a math assignment or a date, after all. It was something about the chemical dump site on the edge of town, near Platt's Corners, so we were treated to a long harangue about that at dinner. A big lecture about poisons leaking into the ground and into our river and so on. And on and on and *on*. I scarcely listened. Boh-ring!

"Remember Love Canal?" she was saying. "That Hooker chemical company buried tons of chemicals. And what happened? Poisons seeped into the ground, into people's houses, into their bodies. Only two of eighteen pregnancies resulted in normal births. Women have had miscarriages, stillbirths, babies with birth defects. That could happen here. It *will* happen, unless someone does something about it."

"Not at supper, please, Wendy," murmured Mom.

37

"Not at supper? When, then? You don't ever want to hear anything unpleasant, anything true. You want to keep living in your own little comfortable soft easy world. You have to wake up, look around, see what's happening. Does it ever occur to you that AnnTanny isn't the only one in this town who's had miscarriages? There have been more in the last five years than in the past thirty. Why? Is there any connection between that and the chemical dump outside of town? Can't anyone put two and two together? Doesn't anybody care? Isn't anybody interested?"

Dad put his fork down. "Your mother's right, Wendy. We can talk after supper."

"Always after! Never now!"

Oh, yecch, I wanted to say. Shut up.

Mom tried to change the subject. "That Clay Priestly seems like a nice boy. Wouldn't you like to ask him over for supper some time?"

Wendy made a disgusted sound. "He wouldn't know what to talk about around here. He's interested in what's happening in the world. About the chemical dump site, for instance, at Platt's Corners. He *cares*. Which is more than I can say about anyone else in this stupid town. We're writing letters to the paper about it. Do you know that—"

The broken record. I wanted to ask her why she didn't just make a tape of everything she had to say and play it over and over, save her strength. Talk about pollution!

What about noise pollution, nerve pollution?

"You have to *do* something," insisted Wendy.

Mom's Great Chicken Wonder *was* great, but how could we enjoy it with Wendy zeroing in on the disasters of the world?

"Look, sweetie," said Dad. "There's not much I can do about saving the world from destruction and disaster. I'm just one small person working in one small bank in one small town."

"In one small insignificant world, right?" asked Wendy angrily. "After all, if the world disappeared, if it went up in grime and smoke and chemicals, it wouldn't make much of a hole in the universe. So it really doesn't matter all that much, does it?"

"Now, now, Wendy," said Dad. "Don't get carried away."

Wendy leaned forward, her hair coming loose and falling over her sharp features, her angry eyes. "Look, Dad, if there's something you can do, you have to do it. So you can't do anything about sunspots, or about black holes, but there's a whole world out there that needs help, and you can do your share. You have to start somewhere. You have to, we all have to, or it's going to be too late. You have to say and do, not just watch and listen. You have to, Dad, you have to."

Dad pushed his plate aside. He'd hardly eaten any of the chicken. Or the zucchini, his favorite. "I'm just doing the best I can in the best way I can," he said quietly.

"Raising a happy family. Having a good honest life. Making everything work."

"It isn't enough!" Wendy brushed her hair back, pulled it tight, twisted it so it wouldn't fall again. "It isn't business as usual, Dad! You can't go along with everyone else who says it is."

"I go along with what I believe in, sweetie," said Dad. "And that's just what life is all about. My life, anyway. Doing the best with what you've got, making your way the way you feel is right, according to your own lights."

Wendy blinked back tears. Tears! "That's what I'm doing. I have to do what I feel is right. I have to stop what I feel is wrong."

Dad looked tired. No wonder: arguing with Wendy would wear out the strongest man.

"There's not one of us who can stop the wrongs of the world," he said.

"That's absurd!" cried Wendy. "One voice, added to other voices—that's the way civilization started, that's what's kept it going, that's the way we can save it now!"

Dad leaned back. "If we all just lead our lives in the most decent way we know, we'll be doing the best we can."

"That isn't enough!" cried Wendy. "The sheep following the sheep, the lemmings on a grand suicide parade! Wave the flags, blow the bugles, beat the drums—here comes the suicide march!"

Oh, wow, she was off again. A one man—one woman —Disaster Squad.

The evening was ruined, as always, because of Wendy. Mom was tired and disappointed, I could tell. Nobody mentioned the terrific chicken, nobody talked about the cookbook. Or about anything: just the Looming Horror of the End of the World.

I stopped listening and started to play a food game with Cissy so she'd finish her dinner. A bite for Mommy, a bite for Daddy, had long since been replaced with a Star Wars game that really seemed to work, even when —like now—Wendy's loud voice dominated the room.

I started to clear the table. Mom was already in the kitchen, getting a yummy dessert ready.

"You get ready, Mom, for AnnTanny. I'll finish up."

"We'll have dessert first," said Mom. "If only Wendy could let us eat in peace for a change."

"That day will never dawn," I told her, carrying in the desserts.

Wendy shoved her dessert aside scornfully. Good: I'd have two.

"I don't suppose either of you would be interested in reading my letter to the editor," Wendy said coldly.

Notice that she said *either* of you, not *any* of you. She'd classed me with Cissy: not old enough or bright enough to understand.

Mom sounded apologetic: "I promised Annie I'd go

over and help her make the curtains for the nursery."

Wendy registered boredom and disgust: she was very good at that. I'd tried to analyze it: the disapproving curve of the lip, the sideways downgrading glance, the smothered exclamation of impatience.

"I'd love to read your letter, honey," said Dad, trying to be interested, trying to be nice, trying, I knew, to smooth things over, to sound enthusiastic, to be a good father. I knew he'd rather relax with the sports page than anything else in the world.

Apparently Wendy was planning to send this letter, like all the others she had written this spring, to the local newspaper. They never printed them, so she had a very low opinion of the editorial staff.

As soon as she'd gone upstairs to get her letter to the editor, I whispered to Cissy, "Come on, let's sneak a Marshomelt!" We tiptoed out to the kitchen, giggling, looking over our shoulders, pretending to be spies stealing important documents. If we were discovered we'd be beheaded.

Then we walked Mom part way to AnnTanny's. We couldn't go in, of course, because I was still contagious. And AnnTanny was positive that Cissy was a carrier of my cold and maybe rabies or something. I wondered if, when AnnTanny's baby was born, she'd keep it in one of those plastic bubbles so no one could get near it. A safe plastic wrapper, a safe plastic baby.

I felt like walking over to Bruno's Palace, but I knew

it was closed. Maybe I could go to Jill's, but I knew she had to study. As usual. I felt like—like what? I wasn't sure. A summer-soft evening should be used, used some way, somehow special, because it *was* special, a lump-in-your-throat kind of time, time for the blues.

Cissy and I had our Marshomelts outside. It was still light and summer warm. We sat on the back steps and then I played hopscotch with her—I'd promised.

I don't know why I was feeling lonely and kind of depressed. Maybe it was just that time of year, just that time of day, so quickly over you felt you had to grab it and use it because it wouldn't come again.

Hopscotch. Wendy was right, I have the mind of a four-year-old child.

The thing was, I wasn't four years old all the way through.

Growing up had advantages and disadvantages. One of the disadvantages was that at times like this you knew you wanted something, but you couldn't figure out just what it was. It's easier to be four and know for sure what that gnawing, restless feeling is. For instance: yep, it's jelly beans I'm in the mood for, not apple pie.

When we came back in, Dad had apparently just finished reading Wendy's letter to the editor. He was nodding thoughtfully, and she was pacing around the living room like a caged tiger. Neither of them paid any attention to Cissy and me. Even Buggsy didn't notice that we had come in.

Cissy went over to the couch to get her dolls; she'd be getting them ready for bed now.

"It's very interesting," Dad was saying cautiously. "And I can see that you've put a lot of time and effort into all your research, honey. But you'll have to sugar-coat and simplify your message, sweetie, or nobody's going to read it. People just don't want to hear a bunch of facts. They'll tune you right out. Change the channel."

"They *have* to listen," insisted Wendy.

"Nobody *has* to do anything but die," said Dad. It was one of his favorite sayings.

"And they will die if they don't start paying attention! The whole world will die! People have to wake up, they have to care!"

I could hear Dad's patient sigh all the way across the room. "Everybody's got an ax to grind, sweetheart. Everybody's got a tale to tell. Everybody wants an audience. You got yourself a whole lot of competition."

Wendy stood still, pushed her sweater sleeves up to the elbows, skinned her hair farther back, and hooked her thumbs in her jean pockets: her arguing position.

Buggsy hid under the couch. Dad looked as if he'd have liked to do the same thing.

"You make it sound as if I were just trying to sell another mousetrap. We're talking about life and death!"

"Look, honey, you asked for my advice about your letter and I'm telling you what I think. This is pretty slow

44

reading. Listen, for instance, to this, sweetie." He picked up Wendy's pages and read:

> "Ninety percent of the 96 billion pounds of hazardous waste generated by American industry is disposed of improperly. . . . This state is the nation's second largest producer of dangerous industrial wastes. . . . Each year we produce 3.8 metric tons of it. . . . And we here in Wellsburg have one of the 34,000 hazardous waste dump sites in the United States at Platt's Corners. What are we going to do about it?

Now who's going to want to read that? No one. You've got to simplify it. Who wants to read a bunch of statistics? You have to make it easy to understand."

"Why should everything be made easy? What are brains for, anyway?" Wendy looked as though her own were going to explode.

"Don't fly off the handle just because I give you advice."

"I should have known better asking you to read it. Nobody in this house, in this town, in this whole stupid world reads anything, knows anything, nobody cares. What did you do all day? Golf. And Mom: practically a whole day at the beauty parlor. And now, fussing around with curtains. *Curtains!*"

She grabbed the paper from Dad's hands. "The world

is falling apart and all you and Mom or anyone else can think about is golf and business as usual."

Dad put up his hand. "Now wait a minute, young lady. Don't get carried away. All I'm saying is that you've got to make this easy to read or no one will bother."

"It's hard to be easy!" shouted Wendy, storming out of the room.

Dad sighed and leaned back. "It's hard to tell that girl anything. Gets mad at the drop of a hat. *It's hard to be easy.* What's that supposed to mean?"

Cissy reached up and pulled my head down. "I love you, Dodie," she whispered. She hated arguments, Buggsy hated arguments. The only one around here who craved fireworks and tension was Wendy.

Dad stood up and stretched. "I suppose she'll sit up there and sulk all night. Make all the rest of us feel guilty. Well, I'm darned if I'll feel guilty." He looked at his watch. "When's Mom coming home?"

"Nine thirty, ten," I told him.

"You'll get Cissy settled and everything?"

"Sure." What else was there to do?

"Then I think I'll go down to the darkroom and print some pictures, get my mind quieted down, okay?"

"Don't worry, Dad."

"Don't you."

"Come on, Cissy, I'll race you upstairs."

Chapter 4

We had two bathrooms upstairs. I always gave Cissy her bath in Mom and Dad's because I had to walk through our room to get to ours, and that usually meant confronting Wendy.

I was just lifting Cissy out of the tub when Wendy walked in. She didn't say anything, just opened the medicine cabinet and took out a bottle of aspirin.

"Using a man-made product," I said in a shocked voice.

"Shut up," said Wendy. "I'm sick."

Sick. Well, if she was sick it was because all that anger inside her had finally poisoned her system.

I listened to her slamming and banging around while I finished getting Cissy ready for bed. I read her two books and told her one story, and by then she was sleepy.

I always listened to Cissy's prayers:

Now I lay me down to sleep,
I pray the Lord my soul to keep.
Bless all the poor and sick and sad,
and make the happy still more glad . . .

"Is Wendy sick, Dodie?"

"I guess so."

So Wendy was sick. Well, that would keep her upstairs and that would keep the downstairs quiet and tranquil.

Now what to do? When in doubt, I usually called Jill. I picked up the phone.

Jill always answered, just the way I always did at our house.

"This is the Department of Water, Gas, and Other Natural Resources," I said. "We are shutting off all water supplies until further notice. Please fill all available bathtubs, pails, bottles, and sinks immediately. Your telephone is now being disconnected."

"Just what I needed," said Jill. "I was going bananas trying to figure out this math junk."

"Want to come over, pop some popcorn, play some junky records, watch a super movie, die of happiness?"

"Wish I could but I can't," said Jill. "Got to finish this stupid math assignment."

That's what you get if you're bright. You get shoved into accelerated classes and you're clobbered with homework. I could hardly remember the last time I'd really done any serious studying at home.

"You're a workaholic," I told her. "I'm just going to laze around."

"I hate you," she said cheerfully and hung up.

So I had the house to myself: Mom was gone, Dad was in the darkroom for the evening, Cissy was sleeping, and Wendy was sick. A whole long night to do whatever I wanted!

But what was it I wanted to do?

All of a sudden my long wonderful free evening seemed endless and pointless, lonely and boring.

I climbed up and got a packet of jelly beans.

"Hey, Buggsy, how about a game of solitaire?" I picked him up, but he squirmed away.

I was just going to settle for a long TV movie that I didn't want to see when I heard a car driving into the driveway. I opened the back door and looked out.

Jobe. I'd forgotten that he was going to bring over the empty boxes for Mom. The prospects for the evening improved. I turned on the yard light and waved. He waved back and opened the trunk of his car and started to lift out the boxes.

I was glad I'd washed my hair. Not that Jobe ever noticed things like that, at least not about me. But you can't carry on much of a conversation if you know you have lumpy hair. You keep thinking about it instead of what you're saying.

He carried all the boxes into the kitchen. "Where do you think?"

49

"Back hall. Coke?"

"Sure." The conversationalists.

I helped with the boxes and then carried two cans of Coke and one box of pretzels into the living room.

Jobe sat on the couch. I sat in the rocking chair and rocked.

"Wendy's sick," I said.

He raised his eyebrows. "Too bad. Nothing fatal, I presume."

"I'm afraid not." I giggled.

Jobe smiled that smile and reached down for Buggsy, who was rubbing against his legs. Jobe picked him up and rubbed him behind the ears. "Hey, ol' Buggsy, hey," he said. "How've you been, anyway?"

I could hear Buggsy purring all the way across the room. I don't know why that cat liked Jobe so much, but he did. Sometimes I thought he liked Jobe better than me.

"Buggsy isn't his real name," I volunteered. "That's just his nickname."

I waited for Jobe to ask about it, but he kept talking to Buggsy. "You miss me, Buggsy?"

"His real name," I said, "is Buggsy Buggaroo of the Buggaroo Buggs." I'd never told anyone that before, not even Jill. Even Jill would have made fun. Jobe didn't laugh, he just nodded and kept rubbing Buggsy behind the ears. "Hey, Buggsy, hey," he crooned. Buggsy's eyes were half shut and so were Jobe's. In fact they looked sort of alike, sitting there, relaxed and contented. I wondered if Jobe was purring, too. Suddenly I felt like sitting over there on the couch with them, but I didn't. Wanting to do something and then not doing it made me feel holy and also cranky.

"How come you don't have a cat if you like them so much?" I asked.

"I don't like cats especially, I like Buggsy."

"If you like Buggsy, you'd like other cats."

"Nope. Buggsy's the cat for me." He kept rubbing Buggsy behind the ears and Buggsy kept purring.

"You know what Buggsy really is?" I asked. "He's a special representative of the Cat Kingdom, sent to earth to convince cat haters that all cats are wonderful. He turns people he meets into instant cat lovers."

"Hey, Buggsy, hey," murmured Jobe.

The doorbell rang, and Buggsy jumped down from Jobe's lap. Telephones ringing and doorbells buzzing bug Buggsy. He hid under the couch.

"I'm on my way," I yelled.

"Who is it?" Wendy called from her bed of pain upstairs.

Jobe glanced up. "She lives," he said.

When I opened the front door something swooshed down on the porch. Oh. Someone had fastened a rolled-up calendar or something to the doorknob.

I untangled it from the rubber band that was holding it together and started to unroll it as I walked back into the living room.

A long list of names.

"Who is it?" Wendy called again.

Honestly, if she was so interested, why didn't she come downstairs? What was I, Western Union special messenger?

"It's just a bunch of names," I yelled back.

I heard her feet hit the floor and in a minute the stairs. Her hair was all tangled up, standing out in all directions, and her face was kind of pinched together. Heck, maybe she *was* sick. It wouldn't have hurt me to be nice.

She didn't even glance at Jobe. He leaned back on the couch and, since Buggsy had fled, started to rub behind his own ears. I felt like saying, "Hey, ol' Jobe, hey."

Wendy grabbed the thing—it looked like a scroll of some kind—and unrolled it all the way.

"The pledge! They've signed it! Look—there must be a hundred names, maybe more!" Her face was suddenly flushed and happy. I hadn't seen Wendy smiling like that in a long time.

"Look! The whole school must have signed!" She whirled around, waving it in the air. Suddenly she saw Jobe and stopped, surprised. Then: "Look, Jobe, they've signed it!"

Honestly, how many times did she have to say it?

He rubbed his forehead and muttered something. He looked kind of embarrassed. Maybe because he'd never seen Wendy in a bathrobe before. Or maybe because he'd never seen her look happy before.

"Do you know what this means?" Her face was all lighted up. "It means they're listening to me, they're listening, they're paying attention, I've won!"

I still didn't know what it was all about, but that's my usual state. Instead of Wendy's telling me I was too dumb to know what was important, happiness made her kind. "This is what I've been trying to accomplish for months. And I never got anywhere before."

It clicked into place. It must be that thing she'd been trying for weeks to get the kids at school to sign:

AEROSOL SPRAYS DESTROY THE
OZONE LAYER
OF THE WORLD'S ATMOSPHERE

I hereby promise never to use aerosol cans again, and to do all in my power to keep others from doing so.

Sign here:

"Terrific," I said, and I meant it, if it made Wendy happy and easier to get along with. Her personality had suddenly undergone a sea change and it was wonderful to behold.

She turned to Jobe and smiled. Smiled!

"What are you doing here, anyway, Jobe?"

"I brought your mom some empty boxes she wanted," said Jobe, smiling back, lighting the room's dark corners. I bathed in the reflected glory of the exchanged smiles.

I kept looking from one to the other as they kept smiling. Wendy Moffitt, formerly ugly and disagreeable, transformed miraculously into a Regular Person, including a smile! Jobe Kopeck, formerly a Regular Person with an occasional terrific smile, now transformed into an idiot who couldn't stop smiling.

I stopped looking at them and started looking at my feet.

"I've got some phone calls to make and some studying to do, see you later, okay?" she said.

Jobe smiled after her and I kept studying my feet.

"See," said Jobe. "She isn't very sick after all."

"It was psychosomatic," I told him. "She got sick because she didn't get her own way about something, and now she got better because she got her own way about something else."

"In years to come they will discover that all illness is caused by a chemical imbalance in the brain. The chemicals can then be altered and no one will be sick."

"And everyone will live forever and the world will be too crowded," I said.

"We can live on space ships, space towns, space worlds," said Jobe. He sat down on the couch again and leaned his head back. That way his Adam's apple showed up a lot. He really wasn't much to look at unless he was smiling.

"All's well that ends well," said Jobe contentedly. "Wendy's well, anyway."

"Just because she's halfway normal for a couple of minutes, you think she's going to keep on being like that."

"I took a course once in grasping at straws. In fact, I may major in it when I go to college this fall."

This fall!

"Are you going to go to college after all?" I asked casually, my heart flipping over and flopping down to my feet.

This was April. If he went to college, he'd be gone by September. I couldn't picture Bruno's, or the town, or me, without Jobe. I couldn't begin to imagine next year. Or ever. He was just sort of woven into everything. Into my subconscious, into my brain cells.

"Are you really going this fall?" I said again. His eyes were closed.

"Um," said Jobe.

"You said you weren't going to college until you knew what it was you wanted to study," I said. My voice sounded sort of whiny, so I cleared my throat to get the whine out. I didn't want to start sounding like a nag.

Jobe started to look very serious, his high forehead crinkling up into a thoughtful frown. I wondered what he'd look like when he was middle-aged. Furrows and wrinkles like Bruno's, probably—a nice, lived-in face.

"I know I said that and I'll probably say it again, and I'll probably think it again," he said, finally opening his eyes and finally—!—looking at me. "I've got to say things out loud so I can hear myself think, decide whether it's a good idea or a bad idea. Unless I say it, and get an echo back, it doesn't seem to be an idea, it doesn't seem to exist."

He leaned forward, clasping his hands. "Actually, no one has ever proved that ideas exist at all unless they're expressed. Unless they're recorded on the wind."

He squinched his eyes up. Thinking seemed to make his face move around a lot. "So I sort of talk to myself, and of course I talk to Bruno. And to you, naturally, when you're around, and to anyone else who'll listen."

He paused and smiled, and I took a deep happy breath, inhaling the smile and smiling back.

"And Wendy," he went on. "I always like to get her reaction."

My smile froze.

Jobe kept talking, more to himself than to me. "I ask myself a lot of questions. So do you. So does everyone. And I have to answer them, you know. In my own head. Every question has an answer. That's what questions are for. To get those answers, wherever they may be."

I tried to think of any important question I'd asked myself lately, and all I could think of was whether I'd have enough jelly beans to last me. But now I tried to look serious and responsible and thoughtful (and questioning), as long as Jobe was finally looking at me.

"Well," he went on, "late last night I began thinking again about college. The pros and the cons. A big pro, for instance, is that unless I do go away, how can I know for sure whether or not there's something out there that's waiting for me, something I want to spend my whole life doing. I don't want to stay at Bruno's forever, you know."

No, I didn't know; I'd just pictured that he'd always be there. But I didn't say anything. I never cared much what Jobe was talking about as long as he was talking, and talking to me. I kept trying to look very very interested, the way Jill and I had decided we should look if we wanted someone to talk on and on.

It worked, in a way. He could see I was listening, but he could also see (how? did I really *look* dumb?) that I didn't quite understand, so he tried to bring it down to my level: food.

"It's like this, Dodie: How would I know that chocolate was my favorite flavor if I'd never tasted it? And what if there was no chocolate in the town I'd always lived in?"

"You'd never miss it," I said, trying to lean forward, clasping my hands sincerely the way he had a few minutes before. It's hard to lean forward and look sincere if you're in a rocking chair, I decided.

"That's okay for ice cream, Dodie, but not for life," said Jobe.

"Yeah, I guess so." That was my stimulating incisive comment. I leaned back, and I knew my face was its most concerned and interested. I knew because I'd practiced ad nauseam in the bathroom mirror. College. Had Wendy tried to talk Jobe into going this fall? I'd never forgive her.

"You don't have to go away to college to find out what's happening in the world," I said. "You could read and study right here in Wellsburg without ever having to go far away and having all that hassle. And all that expense," I added cleverly. "You could study in the library, the way Wendy does."

Of course the minute I'd said it, I was sorry. Why did I have to bring Wendy's name up, anyway? I'd just got rid of her. And I didn't want to picture Jobe studying in the library, probably with Wendy.

"Yeah," he said. He was picking up my vocabulary. "Wendy is something else again." Was that good or bad? I tried to read his expression, but although his eyes were still open he had looked away from me and was examining his fingernails.

"She sure takes things hard," he said. "But then she'll have plenty of company in college. That's a place and a time and an age when you take things hard. You discover new ideas. You discover causes. You discover yourself."

I made a face. "Wendy doesn't have to go to college

58

to find a cause. Complaining comes easy to her. That's what she's going to be when she grows up: a professional faultfinder. Maybe you need a degree to be a really good one, but she's off on the right track."

He raised his eyebrows at me and his forehead turned into sideways wrinkles. "Maybe you're right," he said. "Maybe it isn't the place after all. It's the age you are, it's the time: it's when you're ready. Ready for a new look at everything. Maybe that's what I'm going through right now, college or no college. Maybe my little inside clock said *Bong!* Time to think, time to notice, time to decide what's important!"

I was so busy looking at his face, looking at his eyes, looking at his mouth, waiting for that smile, that I wasn't paying too much attention, except to the word college. Suddenly I thought, Oh wow. What if Jobe goes to the same college Wendy's going to, the state university.

"If you do go to college, where will you go?" I asked with my most sincere phony smile.

"Don't know," he said. "Haven't really decided anything. I'm just getting *ready* to decide. Maybe I won't go to college after all. Maybe I'll join the army, see the world. Or the air force and fly like a bird. Or the marines. Or maybe I'll be a nuclear weapons expert, blow the world apart."

He ran his fingers through his nervous hair. "Or maybe I'll just get myself a girl."

I kept looking at my feet and wondering how old I'd be by the time Jobe came back to town. Or maybe he'd never come back. And then my life would feel like never-has, never-will.

"Hey, Dodie, you look like a black and white picture of gloom, mostly on the black side. Here we've got Wendy squared away and smiling bright, and now we've got you down in the dumps. Can't win them all, I guess."

I looked up and smiled, and then he smiled that smile.

It wasn't fair that I was still just a kid. He'd be married and settled down by the time I was old enough to be noticed.

Jobe stood up and stretched. "Thanks for the Coke and the conversation. And tell Wendy congratulations again about all the signatures on her petition. Or maybe I'll call her tomorrow, tell her myself."

And maybe I'll disconnect the phone, I thought. Disconnect the phone, disconnect Wendy's connection with Jobe.

Off he went, leaving me to ponder my fate. For the first time in my life, I seriously wished I were Wendy's age.

I was still sitting there brooding when I heard Wendy coming down the stairs. She didn't stop to say hello—I'd thought she might, with all her excitement about the signatures. She just marched through the kitchen, opened the back door, and went out into the night. What ever happened to that good mood?

It wasn't the first time she'd gone out to the yard at

night. What did she do there, all alone? Count the stars? I'd have probably felt like going out there myself if she hadn't been there. I was feeling at loose ends. I should have suggested to Jobe that we sit outside and stargaze, but I never think of anything until it's too late. I settled down in front of the TV set and continued to brood.

I woke up in the night. Wendy was sitting at the window seat, looking out. I wondered what had wakened me. Then I realized it was her clenched fist, hitting the windowsill over and over. I could see her face in profile, her jaw thrust out, her mouth turned down, her hair scraggly.

I turned over and went back to sleep. In the morning, she was still sitting there, hunched up, awake, and staring outside. She seemed smaller, somehow. Maybe she *was* melting down like the Wicked Witch.

Chapter 5

Sunday. Well, Sunday wasn't much different from Saturday. Wendy had gone in to take a bath—using about a quarter of an inch of water, probably. I'd dozed off again, with Buggsy on my stomach. When I woke up a couple of minutes later, Buggsy had disappeared. I started to look under the beds.

That's how I found out about the scroll. The whole thing had been torn in half and crumpled up, scrunched under Wendy's bed. I smoothed it out. Signatures, dozens of them, familiar and unfamiliar names.

It was when I looked at the top of the big sheet that I saw: SIGN HERE IF YOU THINK WENDY IS WEIRD. I stared at it.

What a mean trick, what a lousy thing for them to have done. I looked at the list of names again, picking out the ones I knew.

Poor Wendy. She must have read that part about being weird after she'd come upstairs last night. No wonder she'd wanted to go outside to be alone, no wonder she'd sat up all night brooding. I'd brood, too, if anyone did anything like that to me.

Wendy opened the bathroom door and stared at me sitting on the floor with the big sheet.

"You know what?" I said. "All these kids signed first, and then someone rotten just filled in the top line about you being weird. No one knew what they were signing, they just signed. I'm sure that's the way it was."

She grabbed it from me. "You prying little sneak! It's no business of yours!" If looks could kill, I'd have been burned alive.

"Don't you ever dare touch anything of mine—ever! You rotten spy!"

Talk about mean! If Jobe could see her like this, he wouldn't *ever* want to call her. Why had I let myself feel sorry for her even for a minute?

Buggsy poked his head out from my covers—he'd been on my bed all along.

"And get that lousy cat out of here!" shouted Wendy.

That did it. Yelling at Buggsy, or about him, was worse than anything, worse than the worst thing she could ever do. I picked Buggsy up and stalked into the bathroom. Over my shoulder I said, "No wonder everybody says you're weird!"

As soon as I'd slammed the door I started to cry. And I never cry.

I stood under the shower, letting it soothe me and straighten out all the kinks. I thought of what Jobe had said the night before about people reaching a certain time when an inside clock starts to chime away, alerting you, making you interested in things you'd never been interested in before. It had happened to Wendy, it was happening to Jobe. I wondered if it would ever happen to me or whether I'd go through life not being really excited about anything more important than jelly beans. And Jobe's smile.

I took as long as I dared in the bathroom—Wendy would be knocking down the door pretty soon, I knew. Finally I opened the bathroom door and walked into our bedroom.

I needn't have worried. Wendy was sitting on the window seat, her back to me, still looking out. She didn't turn around.

I tried to remember the way she'd been for those few minutes last night when she'd seen the names on that scroll: flushed and happy and nice. Happy. Now she was back to being herself: the Horrible Harpie.

Mom and Dad were going to the country club for lunch. I was staying with Cissy. A lazy, familiar Sunday.

"Tell me a story, Dodie."
"Okay, what about?"

We were sitting on the couch.

"About Buggsy, and how come he's black and white."

"Okay." I rubbed Buggsy behind the ears to keep him in my lap.

"Once upon a time," I said, "all cats were one color, and the color was pink."

"Pink," said Cissy, snuggling closer to me.

"And a kitten was born to the king and queen of cats, and of course it was a pink kitten."

"A kitten princess," whispered Cissy. "And pink ribbons."

"Yes, and all the cat fairy godmothers came, and they brought beautiful presents. And one of the godmothers hadn't had time to get a present. She felt sorry about that. But she said that instead of a present, the kitten princess could have a wish. One wish."

"I like wish stories," said Cissy.

Buggsy apparently did not, for he jumped down from my lap and disappeared under the couch.

"The godmother said that the kitten princess had until midnight to make her wish. The *stroke* of midnight."

I leaned back and shut my eyes. Where was Wendy? Still upstairs, looking out? Looking out at what? Looking for whom? Knowing that she was in the house made me feel prickly and uneasy.

"Then what happened?" asked Cissy, and I tried to pull my mind away from Wendy.

"Well, the kitten princess thought and thought about

the wish. The more she thought about it, the more she wanted to be a different color. Pink was a pretty color, of course, but—"

"She didn't like having pink eyes," suggested Cissy.

"She couldn't decide what color she wanted to be. Maybe green, or blue, or lavender, or orange, or red, or —or maybe jet black. Or maybe pure white. Yes, those were good colors, strong colors. Black. Or white. But which one? Black or white? White or black?"

Cissy sighed happily. "I like this story."

"Well, it was nearly midnight. The clock was striking twelve. 'Hurry,' said the fairy godmother. 'White,' decided the kitten princess. 'No, black,' she said. The clock struck twelve. And that is how black and white cats started. And that's why Buggsy is black and white instead of pink!"

"Is it a true story?" asked Cissy.

"Sure, if you want it to be."

"If you had one wish, just one, what would it be, Dodie?"

"Um. Maybe living happily ever after."

Wishes and stories. I daydreamed a lot that Sunday afternoon.

School was often boring, but in the spring—so close to the end, but not close enough—it was double dull. Every day lasted a week. I thought summer would probably never come.

Jill and I were walking home from school.

"I can't wait until I'm a senior," she said.

"Me neither." Actually, except for Jobe, I was in no particular rush to get any older than I was right now. This I liked. Once I got to be a senior I'd have to be worrying about what to do with my life.

"That Senior Prom will be something really special this year," said Jill. "They're having a terrific band. Maybe by the time we're seniors there won't be any bands. Maybe by then we'll be in a really huge depression and we'll just have electronic music piped in. Maybe not even that."

"Maybe we'll just have to hum to ourselves," I said.

"Yeah. Maybe by that time all the guys will be drafted and off in some dumb war."

"And we'll all have to dance with each other, girls with girls," I said.

"If we're smart," Jill decided, "we'll start looking right now for somebody who's not going to *be* drafted. Someone with really poor eyes or a bum leg, something like that."

"Someone really disabled," I agreed. "Maybe blind or spastic or something." I started to walk backwards, making faces at Jill. "Don't worry," I said. "Things never seem to get as bad as people say they're going to."

"Yeah, they get worse."

She walked along moodily. "Who's Wendy going to the Prom with?"

Wendy, going to the Prom? It had never crossed my mind. And I was pretty sure it had never crossed hers. Who in their right mind would ever ask Wendy to anything, let alone Senior Prom, the main event of your whole school life?

"Oh, I dunno," I said.

"What about that Saul Hogan? He's cute. And haven't they been seeing a lot of each other? They're always in the library."

"Um," I said.

"Well, isn't he? Cute, I mean. And aren't they going together?"

"Well," I said cautiously, "they study together. Because of the debate thing. They aren't really *dating.*"

"Actually, Saul Hogan has been dating Alice Quinn. I've seen them at the movies twice. Not that they were really seeing much of the *movie.*" She giggled.

I didn't say anything.

"I saw Wendy in Bruno's last week," she said. "She looked kind of sick. Maybe she's jealous of Alice Quinn. Jealousy makes you sick, you know. You can *die* of jealousy."

We'd come to Jill's house. It was the only house in town that had a white picket fence all around, and a gate. And Jill was the only person in town who really swung on a gate, the way they do in old movies. I'd wanted for ages to ask Dad to put up a picket fence and a gate, but

I hadn't because it would look as if we were copying the Spooners, and of course we would be.

But I'd have loved to be able to stand swinging on a gate sometime, talking to someone. In my mind I would see myself, my hair no longer lumpy, laughing softly, swinging back and forth and talking. I never could see who it was I was talking to: someone with a nice smile, kind eyes, a perfect person, as I was, in my daydream.

"I can't wait until I'm a senior and can go." Jill sighed. "All we've got is that stupid Sadie Hawkins."

Well, it's true that it was a far cry from Senior Prom to our kind of dance: we were supposed to dress in silly old clothes, the girls asking the boys. And the music of course was just records or tapes. Amplified to about a zillion decibels. That was so no one would have to carry on a conversation. That's supposed to be very hard to do at our age. The best thing about the Sadie Hawkins dance was that you didn't really have to dance. You could just goof around. I couldn't dance, anyway, not *really*.

"Who are you going to ask to Sadie Hawkins?" asked Jill. She stepped onto the little ledge at the bottom of the gate and sure enough, there she was, swinging on a white gate, smiling, her hair swinging softly in the breeze. Too bad it all had to be wasted on me. I knew she was practicing for when some boy would be walking home from school with her.

Who *was* I asking to Sadie Hawkins?

69

It had to be someone in our same grade, but they didn't have to be in our homeroom, or even in any of our classes. It couldn't be anyone in high school, or in another school—or (thinking of Jobe) out of school altogether. Not that I'd have ever thought of asking Jobe to anything, let alone something so childish. He was years and light-years older. I tried to think of what he'd have looked like at my age: Same smile. Shorter. Most of the boys in class came up to about my shoulder. Shy, probably. Sort of like Al Gussaro.

That was it: Al Gussaro would look a little like Jobe when he grew up. Certainly he'd be taller. And by then he'd have had a chance to work on his smile. As for his eyes, I didn't see much of them because he was so shy. He usually looked at the floor, or at someone's shoulder. He'd get over that, probably, by the time he was Jobe's age.

Al Gussaro. A sort of pre-Jobe? I thought about it for a minute while Jill talked.

"I think I'll ask Mel George," said Jill. "He sits next to me in math and he keeps drawing these hysterical cartoons. Or I might ask John Mewles. He's cute."

"Yeah," I said. John Mewles was a show-off.

"Or maybe Randy Elting."

I could see what she was doing. Mentioning everyone so that she'd have first dibs on asking them.

"I think I'll ask Al Gussaro," I said quickly. Now that I'd said it, I decided that I *would* ask him. Tomorrow, when I saw him in the hall, I'd talk fast: he always looked and acted as if someone invisible was walking right behind him so he wouldn't dare stop.

"Al Gussaro?" asked Jill. "What on earth *for?*"

"Because I want to. He's cute," I said. He *was* kind of cute. And shy. It was because he was shy that I wanted to ask him.

"That hair," groaned Jill. "That stupid jacket. His language."

Well, I could see what she meant about his hair. It was sort of odd. Limp, that's what it was. But then so was mine. So was Jobe's. And the jacket: it was far too big for Al. But he'd grow into it eventually.

"What language?" I asked.

"That's what I mean, what language? He never says anything."

"He's nice," I said. Now I was really going to ask him, for sure.

"Nice? I've heard a lot of weird things about him."

"What sort of weird?" I asked.

Of course, I didn't really know him at all. What if he *was* some kind of creep? What if he was on drugs or something? Or what if he drank and what if he got drunk and passed out or what if he'd just embarrass me by being creepy?

"Oh, just funny. I wouldn't want to see you getting into trouble or anything."

Trouble!

"I'll think about it."

"Okay, but if you don't ask him, I will. Maybe I will, anyway."

"Dibs."

"All right, but watch out. I may steal him away from you."

We laughed and couldn't stop laughing. I really liked Jill. And suddenly I really liked Al Gussaro. And Jobe. And everyone in the whole world. Even Wendy.

Chapter 6

Why did I like this dumpy little town? Because it was the only place I knew. Just the way I liked living in my own body, in spite of its obvious disadvantages. It was where I'd been, so I felt at home. Home is where you've always been.

Complaints, sure.

About the town: too small! not enough excitement! not enough changes! About the body: where to begin? the nose, the feet, the everlasting snuffly cold, the *length* of this bod? But where would I feel easier? Everywhere you went in our town you knew ahead of time what to expect. Who would be there, what it would all look like, feel like, be like. Be like forever, the way you knew how you'd be, forever and ever amen.

I was thinking thoughts like these as I rode my bike out to Bissells' at the far end of town. They'd gone to California to visit their daughter. They were going to be gone another month and I'd promised to water their plants. "Once a week, Dodie. No more than that. No less than that. You must promise. Otherwise I couldn't rest easy."

"Don't worry, Mrs. Bissell. I'll be here every week." And I was.

I didn't like riding bikes all that much, especially mine, which had been fairly lopsided and creaky ever since Dad's car had backed into it the one time I'd forgotten to put it in the garage. And the tires kept fading and therefore so did I.

Who would ever want to live out this far? It was almost like living in the country, only without the advantage of having, for example, a horse. It was just a little house, surrounded by zero. Nice if you wanted to talk to yourself.

I let myself in with the key Mrs. Bissell had given me, watered the plants, and let myself out again. I walked around outside the house as I'd promised I'd do, to make sure the flowers out there didn't need watering or mothering or weeding or cutting.

The willow tree was spring yellow, sort of a neon color, and I walked over. Then I ducked under the long, tender down-falling branches. Then I sat down and leaned against the trunk of the willow and looked at the world through the yellowy green. Then I decided that some day maybe I'd live out of the town, maybe in a place like this, with nothing around. Of course I'd have to have a phone and of course TV and someone to be living with and talking to, but for the first time I understood why Mrs. Bissell wanted to live so far away from everything: you could *think*.

I shifted and got more comfortable. I squinted my eyes: blurry and beautiful. A private place, a private time. Only my own thoughts to think instead of everyone else's.

So: what would I think about, now that I had a chance to think? Move, brain.

I shut my eyes, opening them with the noon siren. Every single day at twelve o'clock it was tested. That way, when doomsday came around, they could be sure the siren worked. Disappointing, to have one that didn't, especially if it really *was* doomsday. In the meantime, of course, you always knew when it was noon, even if you were sitting under a tree out in the country.

Even out here I couldn't think my own thoughts. I tried again opening my eyes, seeing the misty gold and the field beyond. No hills around here: I hadn't seen a hill in years, except on TV. But fields: all planted and ready to go. Planted with what? If you had a choice, what would you choose?

I stretched, thinking maybe stretching my body would stretch my mind. All it did was add an extra inch. But not to my brain.

The noon whistle had reminded my stomach it was

time for something to eat. Jelly beans. That's what I'd plant: jelly bean trees. No, not trees, bushes. Or maybe plants. Maybe they'd grow like corn. You'd peel off the husk and there would be rows of little multicolored jelly beans.

My stomach wouldn't let me think. I got on my bike and rode home, thinking of jelly beans. Face it, once a C person always a C person. I probably didn't even *have* a little inside clock.

Dad had decided to wash the station wagon and Cissy was helping him by splashing in the water and keeping him company. I made some lemonade and I brought some out in paper cups.

"Dodie to the rescue," said Dad when he saw me. Cissy jumped up and down. "Lemoney ade, lemoney ade!"

"The car looks great," I told Dad. "Squeaky clean."

"Well, we can only hope that getting washed and shined a bit will improve its disposition. If not, I'll sell it to the highest bidder come winter."

"Never," I told him. "It would be like selling Buggsy. The station wagon is a part of the family. You can't get rid of a relative just because of old age. Or because of disagreeability," I added, thinking of Wendy.

"Right you are, sweetie," said Dad. "I like your sentimental sentiments."

We did have another car, newer and smaller and more predictable, but we all really liked the old wagon the best. The seat at the back was Cissy's and my favorite place to sit. It faced backwards, so we'd pretend the cars behind us were trying to swallow us, and they would, when they passed us.

Mom hated to ride backwards. She said it was spooky to see where you'd been but not where you were going. "Well," Dad told her, "it's just like life: you can't see ahead."

"Praise the Lord," said Mom.

Wendy and I would take the Ford today; it was our turn to do the marketing.

We always traded: sometimes it was Dad and me, sometimes it was Mom and Dad, sometimes Dad and Wendy, and so on. Cissy comes along when she feels like it.

There's always a list. Mom won't ever buy anything or let us buy anything that isn't on it because that's Impulse Buying.

We divide the list: one of us gets the dairy products, the meat and fresh vegetables and fruits, the other gets the canned goods and bottled and boxed stuff, and then we meet at the checkout counter.

Supposedly two people can do the week's marketing in half the time that it would take one of us to do it, right? Wrong. With Wendy, you had to allow extra time for complaints, arguments, scenes, and threats against the management.

Today I took the dairy things and Wendy took the other list. We each got our own cart and separated.

I could hear her voice all the way across the store, arguing with one of the clerks. This time it was about aerosol cans. I'd have tried to pretend I wasn't with her, but she had the money. Everyone was staring at us as we checked out, and she was demanding to see the manager.

I thought maybe she'd have used up all her energy and anger, but not so. She took one look at the stuff in my cart and started screaming again. "Look at that date on the whipping cream! It's two months from now. Do you know what that means? It means that it's so shot full of preservatives that it's artificial. It isn't even cream, it isn't anything. Dodie, take it back."

And so on. And then the big thing about having all the candy bars and chewing gum right there at the checkout counter so that little kids would see some stupid treat and want it, and probably to avoid any temper tantrums, their parents would buy it, and where was the manager's sense of responsibility, and she was going to write another letter to the higher-ups of this particular chain of grocery stores and see that he got fired if he insisted on continuing this practice, and so on and on and on and on. . . .

The manager, a nice young worried kind of guy with a droopy mustache, came over. He must have been getting sick of Wendy. He looked more and more worried and anxious as she yelled on. He tried to be soothing and mumbled something about "company policy" and "company regulations," and the more he tried to placate her the angrier she became.

"The company store, the company, is that all you think about? Can't you make your own decisions? Can't you see what you're doing, just following orders? Why don't you have the guts to stand up and be counted? Refuse to carry dangerous products, refuse to carry merchandise that you know for a fact is pure junk?

"It's not just that your customers are wasting money, that's bad enough, but you're endangering them, you're endangering the futures of the little kids they're buying for, you're ruining their chances of having a balanced normal diet and a healthy life. It's your responsibility, understand? It's your responsibility, and you can't hide behind the Store Policy!"

"Yes, yes, I understand what you're trying to say," said the manager.

I looked at his plastic name card: A. Magnuson. A for what, I wondered? Adam, Allen, Adolph, Alfred?

He kept talking in a very soothing quiet voice, but he didn't really know Wendy. The more soothing you were, the more excited she became.

"The public wants certain products, and we like to supply them, because of course if we did not, then someone else would, and our store would collapse. Collapse," he repeated anxiously.

"Don't you see what you're doing?" Wendy asked angrily. "If your children asked for poison, would you give it to them?"

A. Magnuson coughed nervously and looked around the store, wondering, I'm sure, how many people were listening. Everyone, of course, because her voice was always pitched at the listening level.

"That's stretching the point," he said in what I thought was a sensible and dignified manner. "And of course I have no children. I'm not married." He cleared his throat. "I see your point," he added. "I see your point. But then, of course, I expect you to see mine."

Good for him. I really liked this guy A.

Wendy stared at him, at first in surprise, and then I think in respect—not because of his point of view, but because he had the guts to talk back to her.

"You have no point of view," she said finally. "You only echo what your superiors say, what they expect you to say. If you quarreled with their approach, you'd lose your job. And after all, your job is the most important thing in the world, isn't it?"

He looked back at her with his big soulful eyes and his big soulful mustache. "I guess it is, in a way. I have to have a job, you know, and this is it."

His voice had fallen to a lower register along with hers, so now it was more of a one-on-one conversation. The other voices in the store rose and fell, rose and fell. Wendy and A. stared at each other for a minute. "You have given me food for thought," he said finally.

"Thank you," said Wendy quietly, looking into his eyes. She must have been tired to have toned down so much. And suddenly she looked kind of pretty. Not as pretty as she used to be, but not as ugly as she'd been in the last year.

A. Magnuson was very smart, I decided, pretending to think about what she was saying. It was the only way he could get her out of the store quietly.

I wouldn't have believed that Wendy could have got any meaner or madder than she was already, but the next few days proved that someone like Wendy could *always* get worse. She sulked and skulked, banged doors and harangued everybody who dared get within six yards of her. I was watching something on TV with Cissy that next afternoon when she barged in: "Don't you ever have any homework to do?" She was home from school early.

"I do it in study hall, not that it's any of your business."

"No wonder you get such dumb grades. You're lazy."

"I'm not lazy, I'm dumb," I said. "Unsmart. But at least I'm smart enough to know I'm dumb."

The TV program was ruined.

Slam, bang, thump. She changed her clothes and came down in old blue jeans and sneakers. I paid no attention to her. She slammed outside. In a few minutes I went out to the kitchen to get some jelly beans and a Coke. I

looked out of the window. She was digging in the yard.
Maybe a grave, I decided.

I found out that night that she'd started a vegetable
garden. She'd often talked about doing that, but never
had before.

"Good," said Dad. "A backyard garden."

I was watching TV with Cissy in the living room, but
I could hear him in the kitchen talking to Mom. "Maybe
having a garden will help to soften her up, tone her
down, get her squared away." He sighed. "Maybe plant-
ing and weeding and hoeing and raking will burn off
some of that angry streak." He didn't sound very hope-
ful.

"It's a good sign," said Mom. "She's never been interested in anything like that before. Back to earth, back to
basics? I wonder." Well, they'd better not get their hopes
up. Once mean, always mean and meaner.

At supper, Wendy started to talk about Mr. McCabe
again, and his spraying, and then on and on about insec-
ticides and pesticides and herbicides. She had appointed
herself a committee of one to purify the world. Now she
was talking about some book.

"How old was I when what was published?" Dad
looked up pleasantly from his plate.

"*Silent Spring*. You know. Rachel Carson's book. I'm
sure you've heard of it," Wendy added icily.

"Of course. Well, I don't know how old I was."

"You were about my age. About *my* age. And what did

you do about it? Nothing. But you could have, that's the point. You could have."

"Well, baby, we can't do something about everything. Certainly not about every single book that's published."

"We're not talking about every *single* book. We're talking about *Silent Spring*. And if you'd cared, if you'd spoken up, if you'd *tried*, if you'd *worked*, if your generation had got together, done something, it wouldn't have been too late. But no, it wasn't *important*. You just sat by and let it all happen! People who don't *care* are a blight, like a fungus, and you—" If I shut my eyes I could see her words, all italicized, and all probably black and blue.

"Wait a minute, young lady," Dad interrupted. "We can't all be movers and doers and shakers and shouters. Why should I feel guilty? Guilty of what? I'm not a robber, not an embezzler, not a rapist, not a murderer—"

"It isn't enough just to do no wrong! It isn't enough!" said Wendy. It was her pre-yelling voice.

"It's enough for Mom and me," said Dad in his closing-the-subject voice.

Wendy didn't take the hint. She thrust her head forward and shouted. "It's enough for Mom and me," she mimicked exaggeratedly. "There you go again, thinking and speaking for Mom. For all you know, she has ideas of her own! Let her talk for herself for once!"

Dad bristled. "And there *you* go again, young lady, grabbing each and every innocent remark, turning it into a subject for a quarrel. Well, I'm good and sick of it, I can tell you! And there'll be no more of it, do you hear?"

Wendy smiled, a tight triumphant smile. "Good for you, Dad. Anger is the first step."

She stood up and walked out of the room, head up, eyes blazing.

Dinner was ruined once again.

People say a quarrel clears the air, but it doesn't. It muddies it, pollutes it, like the chemicals that Wendy is always talking about. One more evening loused up. Now we were all on edge and angry.

Dad put his paper on the floor. "Guess I'll go down and work in the darkroom," he said.

"At least it's quiet down there," I said. "Peaceful."

He smiled. "Don't you ever grow up angry," he said.

"I won't," I promised.

Maybe I'd never grow up at all. I'd just had supper, but all I could think of was those packets of jelly beans, up in the cupboard behind the plates we never use.

Jill had finally decided to invite Randy Elting to Sadie Hawkins, but she needed some moral support and I was it. I hadn't even seen Al Gussaro, not even in the halls, so I hadn't had to decide yet what to do.

"Let's practice me calling Randy," suggested Jill.

"Okay," I said. "Come on over after school."

Mom was sitting in the backyard in a bikini, trying to get a suntan. "I am still working on the new improved me," she called. She was covered with ugly greasy stuff but she still looked pretty.

Jill lay on Wendy's bed. I lay on mine. We pulled the hall telephone on its long extension into the room.

"As soon as I practice a couple of times, I'll call him right from here, cross my heart, hope to die." It was one of our old sayings, one of our old promises: cross my heart, hope to die. What it meant, of course, was, I hope I die if I don't follow through. Kid stuff.

We'd brought up some pretzels and potato chips and a couple of cans of Coke. It was like a million other days. And I could really relax because Wendy wouldn't be home from the library for a couple of hours. I hoped.

"You be Randy and pretend I'm calling you," said Jill. She giggled. "I feel like a spider. Spinning my web, trying to trap some poor unsuspecting fly."

"Spider Spooner," I said, and we giggled helplessly. Buggsy jumped to the floor and took refuge under my bed. He hates noise, even joyful noise.

"Spider Spooner strikes again," I managed to gasp between paroxysms of laughter. My sides ached but I couldn't stop laughing at my cleverness. Jill put a pillow over her face. "Simmer down, Spider," I said, and we were off on another laughing jag.

Finally Jill wiped her eyes, took a breath, sat up, and said, "Now let's be serious."

"Serious Spider."

She giggled. "Let's practice. I'm calling. You're Randy."

"Okay."

Buggsy decided things were going to be more tranquil and jumped back up on my stomach. Jill cleared her throat. "Here goes. You're Randy and your telephone is ringing."

"One ringy dingy," I said, and started to giggle. Jill frowned at me. She was taking this very seriously all of a sudden.

"Hello," I said.

"Hello, Randy."

"This isn't Randy, this is his mother," I said cleverly.

"Oh." Jill stuck out her tongue at me. "Well, is Randy there?"

"Yes, he's here."

Jill frowned at me. "Be serious," she whispered. She took a breath. "Could I speak to him, please?"

"I'll see if I can rouse him," I said, smiling at my witty remarks. "You're the sixteenth girl who's called him today and the poor lamb is utterly exhausted, and I do mean utterly, and I do mean exhausted."

We laughed for a while after that, finished off the pretzels and the Cokes, and I went down for more cans and some jelly beans.

A couple of other rehearsal tries: "Yes, this is Randy and I've got the measles and I'm contagious and did you know that germs are transmitted through telephone wires?"

Jill shrieked with laughter. No wonder she'd been my

best friend for so long; she always laughed at my feeble attempts at humor.

Finally she screwed up enough nerve to place a real call. There was no answer.

"And I was all psyched up." Jill sighed.

"Well, call someone else," I suggested. "After all, Randy Elting isn't the only pebble in the ocean."

"He isn't the only fish on the beach," she said.

"He isn't the only fly in the soup."

"He isn't the only bat in the belfry."

"He isn't the only pea in the pod."

"He isn't the only bee in the bonnet."

We started laughing again, and Buggsy jumped off the bed and stalked out of the room. He'd had all the laughing he could take.

"Why don't you call someone?" asked Jill. "You still thinking of asking that Al Gussaro?"

"Maybe," I said. Calling someone on the telephone wasn't my idea of the way you'd go about inviting someone to something, though. I'd ask face to face. On a telephone, you don't know who else is on the other end and what's happening and you can't see their face and you can't talk to a disembodied voice. Silences are enormous on a telephone. But when you can *see* someone, talking isn't all that important; you can fill in the empty spaces trying to find something in your pocket, or looking over your shoulder at something, or brushing something off your shirt, or tying your shoe.

"Let's go to Bruno's, have some pie," suggested Jill.

I hesitated. I wanted to go to Bruno's, but not, I decided, with Jill. Not today. Our giggling over Randy Elting and Sadie Hawkins seemed suddenly silly and childish. If I was ever going to grow up, now was a good time to begin. But I remembered that my only reason for wanting to grow up at all was Jobe. So he wouldn't outgrow me.

"Why don't we go to your house, pop some corn, try Randy again?" I suggested.

"Okay." She was as easy as Cissy to get along with.

Eating popcorn, watching TV, lying on the floor, giggling—even when I grew up, I could still do things like that. I didn't have to be a student, or a scholar, or a doer, or a millionaire, or anything. I didn't have to go to college to learn a lot of stuff. I could just *be.* Anything wrong with that?

"With what?" asked Jill. I hadn't realized I'd said it out loud.

I wished I'd had a sister like Jill instead of Wendy, and I wished it even more when I walked back into our house.

Mom and Dad were in the kitchen with Wendy. Wendy was sizzling dangerously; if you'd touched her you'd have been electrocuted.

"I won't do it," she said. "I won't. I don't care what they say, I won't."

I wondered what had set her off. Of course it didn't take much, it was like a match tossed in a long-parched tinder-dry forest. Suddenly—wham-o!

"Tell us about it," Dad said in his most controlled pleasant voice. Cissy climbed down from Dad's lap and I wondered if he wished that Wendy would take her place. She needed a good rocking. Or a good spanking. But of course she'd get neither.

"I told you. Dr. Somers just called. I'm supposed to debate *for* nuclear power. For!"

She looked wildly around the room as if she expected it to explode. Dad cleared his throat. "Well, as I understand it, sweetie, there are two sides to every question. And you've been assigned one side."

"And that nice Saul Hogan the other," said Mom helpfully. She was doing something at the stove. "Maybe he'd trade with you."

"That isn't allowed," said Wendy. "It's against stupid Dr. Somers' stupid rules."

"Well, rules are rules," said Dad reasonably. "Those were the rules of the game when you started. You can't back out now."

"You don't understand!" shouted Wendy. "I can't argue in favor of something I'm against!"

"It's only a high school debate, after all, sweetie. The world isn't going to come to an end if you take the side you don't want. It isn't that important."

"Important!" yelled Wendy, her face a tight mask. "Remember Three Mile Island?"

"Well, all of that was greatly exaggerated. Nothing

much really happened, no one was injured, no one died, it was a lot of fuss over a minor accident."

"You can't believe that! Don't you understand? We're arguing about life and death while you sit around! This is the world's future we're talking about. There's no second show, no rerun, no instant replay, no other chances. This is it, I-T, the one and only main event."

"Well, now," Dad said, "you're putting more into it than there really is. Calm down."

She didn't even hear him.

"There's no twice, Dad. No second chance. You're not watching a show, you *are* the show. It's happening. It's happening and you're letting it happen. You're just sitting there, letting everything wash over you. A stone can do that much. But we're not stones, we're people, living, breathing, thinking people. We're all in this together, we're all living at the same time, today, now. And everyone is thinking that someone else will take charge, someone else will yell fire, someone else will bring the ladders and the hoses. Someone else. But not you, oh, no, not any of you."

She stopped, out of breath.

Dad put his hand up to his head. Zapp, biff, bam, and our prospects for a nice relaxed easy evening had gone up in smoke.

"Look, doomsayer," said Dad. "Lots of bad things could have happened that never did happen at all. Lots of people at one time or another for hundreds of years have thought that the world was going to end. And it doesn't end, sweetie, it doesn't. It never has, and it never will. Not for a billion years, anyway. And by then it won't matter to any of us. Not even to you, honey, not even to you."

Wendy turned and ran. Not upstairs this time, but out to the kitchen and *(slam)* outside. Hers was the only voice she wanted to hear.

Mom, who had been stirring something yummy on the stove, turned around. "Arguing with her just upsets you. And her. And it never does any good."

"I know." Dad sighed. "You can just try to put the brakes on, I guess, try to keep her from knocking her head against the wall."

So: Wendy had refused to debate. What about poor Saul Hogan of the startling eyes? What was he supposed to do without a partner, without an opponent? He'd worked on all that research as hard as she had. Harder, because he didn't have to stop every few minutes to yell at someone.

And Dr. Somers. What about his debate program? Wendy was a lousy sport, ruining everything for everybody. She could write a book: *How to Make New Enemies and Still Keep the Ones You've Got.*

Chapter 7

All of us had chores, and we rotated them. This time it was my turn to fold the laundry, Wendy's turn to empty the wastebaskets.

Suddenly I remembered that the wastebasket in our room had about ten empty nonbiodegradable jelly bean packets in it. My insides turned from rosy red to pale, quivering Jell-O as I pictured the scene ahead.

It would be simpler to empty the wastebaskets myself than to listen to another scream session. Luckily Wendy was outside, fussing around in her garden.

I ran down to the kitchen and got a big plastic bag. I'd get every single wastebasket emptied before she came back in the house, and then I'd get the big plastic bag out of sight, because otherwise she'd start yelling that *it* was nonbiodegradable.

First, our room. I turned the wastebasket upside down.

Yep, there were the jelly bean packets. And gum wrappers, empty pop cans, and lollypop sticks—lucky I'd decided to be the one to do the wastebaskets. I started dumping. There were lots of little torn pieces of colored paper in the basket, too. Our pads of paper. One pink one caught my eye: there was writing on it, and the writing was Wendy's, and the word was *passion.* I set the wastebasket down and plucked out another piece of paper—this was pale green. And I read: *belong to you forever.* A blue one: *this raging love, this aching need, I never . . .*

I crouched there, stunned.

No wonder Wendy had become so impossible: Wendy was in love!

My pulse raced, my mind reeled, my body was congealed with excitement and indecision. I absolutely had to put those pieces together. It wasn't like sneaking or spying, and it wasn't dishonest. I'd be putting together the pieces of Wendy, understanding her, and unless and until I understood her I couldn't help her.

I picked up one more torn piece: *. . . are my love, my life, my . . .*

Then I tossed everything into the big plastic bag. Where could I go where I'd be private? The bathroom. I'd already washed my hair, but I'd pretend I was washing it again. That would give me time, time at least to get all the torn pieces. I could put them together later. I carried the bag into the bathroom with me and locked the door. Then I turned on the water, sat on the floor, and dumped everything out of the bag. It took only a few minutes to sort it all out. The fact that they'd been written on all different colors of sheets would make it easy to put them together. Some of them were too tiny and crumpled to read, but there were enough.

A pounding at the door.

"Do you know how much water you're wasting?" shouted Wendy.

I pretended not to hear, but she pounded again, so hard I thought she might knock down the door.

"Turn off that water, stupid!" she yelled.

Somehow I felt kinder about Wendy now, knowing that she was suffering the pangs of love. I turned it off.

"Do you know how many gallons you waste every time you wash your hair?"

"Okay, okay," I said. "It's off, stop bugging me."

Who was Wendy in love with?

I gathered together all the pieces and crammed them into the pockets of my jeans. I'd have to put them together later.

I wrapped a towel around my head and picked up the big trash bag. I'd find a private place and put the puzzle together. Wendy in love: incredible.

Who? Who was it?

I suddenly realized that there was nowhere in the whole house except the bathroom where I could be private. And even the bathroom, with Wendy banging on the door every second, wasn't too terrific. I had to find a place where I couldn't be interrupted. I had to read those notes.

Wendy in love! Saul Hogan! Who else? She never saw anyone after school but Saul, and now, of course, after the debate fiasco, she didn't even see him. She was pining away. That's why she'd been so cranky all these months.

I suddenly remembered what Jill had told me: Saul had been dating Alice Quinn. So: Wendy's heart was broken. She probably had refused to debate with him just to get even. So she'd cut off her nose to spite her face because now she'd *never* see him, and Alice Quinn would have him all to herself.

I had to put those pieces together, I had to. Where could I go where I'd be safe?

The darkroom. The only private place in the house. Dad wouldn't be home until five, I'd have plenty of time. Mom was over at AnnTanny's with Cissy.

I ran down the basement stairs.

There wasn't a lock on the darkroom door. Too bad.

What if Wendy decided to barge in all of a sudden and found me with all these scraps of paper, all these love notes?

Well, I'd be able to hear her coming down the stairs. I'd have time to scoop the papers into a drawer, out of the way, out of sight.

I turned on the light and shut the door. I emptied my

pockets and smoothed all the pieces out on the counter. Now: where to begin?

I picked up a pale green corner: *love would be.* There were about a dozen green ones. If she'd written on both sides it would take forever. She had.

I must have been down there for half an hour, and I still hadn't put the pale green ones together. This was proving to be a harder job than I'd thought because there were two different notes written on green.

It took another half hour before I could really read anything:

> Searching for I knew not what
> I stumbled blindly into love
> and at that blessed instant knew
> that this was love
> to last and last forever
> and love would be
> my burden and my wings

Well, it didn't make much sense, but it was enough to prove to myself that Wendy was really in love. Saul Hogan, with those irresistible eyes. You could hardly blame her. Or that Alice Quinn. Or anyone. If it hadn't been for Jobe, I'd probably have been daydreaming about Saul.

Voices: Mom and Cissy were home. But maybe there was time to figure out the rest of the green pieces before

I was discovered. Now that I had only a few green ones left, it wouldn't be too hard.

"Dodie, where are you?" It was Cissy.

And Dad would be coming home soon. This would have to be the last one until after supper.

> I close my eyes
> against the bright of you
> the magic light of you
> you are too much to bear
> I love you so
> I close my eyes

I remembered the way they'd studied at the dining room table, Wendy with her nose in the books and papers, never glancing up, never looking Saul in the eyes; she was afraid she'd drown in them. She had, anyway.

I'd Scotch-taped all the notes together. But where to hide them? Up with the jelly beans? In my big shoulder bag? How private was that, really? "Dodie, can I count your pennies?" "Dodie, I'm just going to take a dollar from your purse for the paper boy. I'll pay you back when I go upstairs." "Dodie, do you have any chewing gum in there?" That last was Jill.

I'd never realized before that I didn't have any privacy, I'd never even known I needed any. I was terrified that Wendy would find me out. My life would be over. I thought about confiding in Jill, but this was too personal, too private. I couldn't let anyone else know that Wendy was in love. *Tragically* in love; why else would she be so miserable *all the time*? When love was a two-way street, it only made you happy, I knew *that* much. I read *some* things. And of course you learn a lot from watching television. Finally I put all the Scotch-taped notes into my shoulder bag, behind the zippered pocket. I'd carry it with me or keep it in sight.

Wendy wasn't going to Senior Prom. No surprise.

"But, dear, you're a senior, and Senior Prom, after all is—" said Mom anxiously.

"I've said I'm not going, and I'll say it again. I'm not going. It doesn't mean anything." That sentence sounded familiar, but then most of what Wendy said was a repeat performance of something else.

Didn't Mom ever consider the obvious fact that probably no one had invited Wendy? That no one wanted to take her anywhere, or be seen with her? Who in the world wanted to subject themselves to an evening of battle? Senior Prom was long dresses and corsages and pretty hair and perfume and laughing and flirting and having a fancy supper, before or after. And, I suddenly thought, maybe Saul Hogan had asked Alice Quinn to Senior Prom. Of course.

I wondered vaguely how long my feet would be by the time I was a senior. And who I'd be going to Senior Prom with, when the time finally rolled around. It had to be another senior, which meant it had to be someone in my class now. New people hardly ever move into town. Jobe was the first and only one in ages. I thought about it and finally came back to Al Gussaro. Maybe if he worked on his shyness and his smile and his hair and his conversation and his clothes and his height for a few years, he'd be okay by then. And by then maybe I'd be ten feet tall and he'd have to bring along a ladder.

I was just opening my locker at school and thinking about Al Gussaro when I saw him coming down the hall, head bent. He slowed down when he came closer—he'd probably seen my feet. I took a deep breath and said, "Hey, Al." He glanced up and glanced back down again. The most fascinating thing about me was my feet, I decided.

"Hey," he said.

"Want to go to Sadie Hawkins with me? We wouldn't have to dance, just goof around, watch everybody, have a Coke."

"Yeah," he said, finally dragging his eyes up to my chin. My chin: I'd never really thought about my chin before, and wondered now if it was really prominent or really receding or whether it had a smudge on it or maybe a pimple. I hadn't checked.

"Well, would you like to?" I asked, and finally his eyes got up to my nose which suddenly started to itch like crazy. I scratched it while he watched, and finally his eyes met mine. Good: nice eyes, even with the glasses. And finally he smiled: nice, good smile, even with the braces. And finally he said, "Sure, let's."

"Okay," I said, fumbling with the locker.

"Okay." And his eyes were back on the floor again. It didn't matter, I had a date. My first real date. Well, Sadie Hawkins wasn't a real date, and after all *I'd* had to ask *him,* but to myself I was going to call it a date. I pictured a big album and on the cover was printed—or engraved; yes, it was an important album, after all—DODIE'S DATES. And on the first page: Al Gussaro. And a picture. And then on the last page a picture of my wedding, years later, to someone or other, and in between pages and pages of all the dates I'd have had.

My life was just getting started. I was going to be growing up now.

On the way home from school, I said, "I asked Al Gussaro."

"No kidding," asked Jill. "What did he say?"

"He said sure."

"So now we both have dates. Want to go together? Dad could drive."

"Sure."

We walked to Jill's house. She stepped on the gate and started to swing. I wondered where Al Gussaro lived and whether he ever walked this way. Then I wondered if Jobe ever walked this way.

"Funny no one else had asked Randy or Al Gussaro," said Jill.

"They were saving themselves for us," I told her, and we giggled hysterically.

Another supper! It seemed to me we were always sitting at the table, holding our breath, waiting for Wendy to pounce. I was almost afraid to look at her tonight for fear she'd see that I knew her secret. She sat, hunched over, playing with her food.

What if Saul Hogan would call her, right now? What if he'd say, "Look, Wendy, I've been a fool. Let's get together. Let's stay together. Let's go to Senior Prom together. Let's live happily ever after."

I tried to picture her face if that happened. I tried to push my mind back all those months to remember what she used to act like, look like, sound like, *be* like.

Come on, Saul, I breathed silently. Come *on*. When the phone rang, I jumped. But of course it wasn't Saul.

It was Clay Priestly.

Clay Priestly. When Wendy went upstairs to answer the telephone I concentrated on trying to hear what she said. A soft voice. No anger. Just easy. Just—love?

When she came back downstairs she seemed happy. Or as happy as Wendy could be, these days. Not really smiling, but looking as if she *could* smile. Had they quarreled and then made up? Which one was Wendy really in love with?

After supper the phone rang again. This time it was

Jobe, wondering if we wanted any more empty boxes for Mom's attic-sorting spree.

"Besides, I want to take a look at that garden of Wendy's," said Jobe.

"It isn't much so far," I told him. "Just invisible seeds."

"I'm going to put in my order now for juicy tomatoes in juicy tomato season."

I'd have started a garden myself, if I'd thought Jobe would be that interested. How had he found out about Wendy's?

I puttered around in the kitchen after supper and made some fudge and looked out the window. Mom and Dad had gone out with Cissy for a drive in the country. I called Jill: no answer.

Of course when Jobe finally came, he spent almost the whole time admiring Wendy's garden and talking to her. A waste of time! I wanted to call: She's thinking about Clay Priestly! Or Saul Hogan! She doesn't even know you're alive, you dope!

They came in the house together. Working in the garden had put some color into Wendy's cheeks. She washed her hands at the kitchen sink, threw water on her face, and rubbed it dry. It almost glowed.

"Remember, my friend, it's a promise about the tomatoes," said Jobe, smiling at her.

"I'll remember," said Wendy. How come she was so pleasant all of a sudden?

I might as well have been down in the darkroom the whole time. Jobe and Wendy talked about the garden. The carrots, the lettuce, the onions, the bell peppers, the beets. Boring! I sat in the rocking chair and held Buggsy, and felt like a wallflower. I felt horrible.

I went upstairs, carrying Buggsy and my shoulder bag with me. They didn't even notice. Jobe was telling Wendy how to stake tomato plants.

Maybe when I left the room they'd start talking about college. Maybe they *would* go to the same one and maybe they'd be college sweethearts and maybe then I'd just die.

I took the notes and went into the bathroom and shut the door. I read every single note over one more time:

> You are my love, yes
> but more than that, a friend.
> Friend: in my lexicon
> the word means: forever
> and I am forever yours.

I sat there staring at Wendy's handwriting through the Scotch tape. At least, I think it was the Scotch tape that made everything look blurry.

It wouldn't be Jobe. It couldn't be. It wasn't fair!

Wendy and I were at the supermarket: it was our turn. The last couple of times, she'd insisted on going alone: bliss.

I knew she'd be complaining. This time it was the green peppers, and how they'd been sprayed with something horrible just so they'd look shiny. A. Magnuson came hurrying over, trying to avoid another shouting match. Suddenly, seeing them talking together there at Fresh Fruits and Vegetables, I saw with a sudden burst of knowing: it wasn't Saul Hogan or Clay Priestly after all. It was A. Not Jobe! Not Jobe!

My jaw dropped. A.! That's why she'd been going to market alone lately!

Of course. All those times in the supermarket, all those arguments. Her demanding to see the manager, just so she could complain. When what she really wanted was to see him, just to talk to him, just to be around him, maybe get well enough acquainted so he'd ask her out. Well, Wendy my friend, that's not the way to get a guy. Absolutely not. The way to get a guy—

And yet there he was, drinking it all in, nodding and talking back. Talking back! Staring her down—or trying to, anyway.

Well!

"I wonder what his name is," I said on the way home. "Maybe Aloysius. Maybe Agamemnon. Maybe just plain Al."

"Who? What are you talking about?" she demanded. But she knew.

"The manager. A. Magnuson."

"Oh. Well, why don't you ask him?"

Clever. Pretending she didn't know.

"I will. Next time," I said.

The rest of the way home was devoted to complaints about spraying, about additives, about packaging, about (oh, yes) aerosol cans.

I didn't even listen to her. I never did, but this time I didn't even hear her, I was so excited about knowing or hoping that Wendy was in love with A. Magnuson!

Saturday. And school was almost over. I could hardly wait.

Dad and Mom had taken Cissy over to visit AnnTanny and Uncle Frank. Wendy was in and out, out and in, yelling at me every time she saw me. She was crabbier than ever, if such a thing was possible.

I wanted to say, "I know why you're like this, you're in love!" But I didn't.

The Saturday paper always came early. Wendy had grabbed it an hour earlier and had practically torn it apart, looking at it. I knew her letter to the editor would never be published; they never were.

I picked up the paper to read the comics and to see my horoscope for the day. And there was a familiar face staring out at me. An owlish sort of man. Then I remembered: Dr. Ellis Somers. I read the article. He was leaving town. Accepting a terrific post in a college in the East. Well, great.

But suddenly something rang a bell. I leaned back in

the kitchen chair and shut my eyes. Dr. Somers. And the little notebook of his that Wendy had kept. I reached for my shoulder bag and fled to the bathroom, locking the door.

> A part of you
> belongs to me
> a tiny part, a part I stole
> a part so small
> it scarce exists, except for me
> into that part
> I pour
> enough of love to fill the whole

Dr. Somers. Possible, possible. Anything was possible, anyone. Anyone but Jobe.

I woke up in the night with my cold. I'd been dreaming about Wendy, dreaming that she was getting smaller and smaller.

I listened, but I didn't hear her breathing. I sat up. Her bed was empty. She wasn't in the bathroom, either. Maybe she'd had a bad dream, too, and had gone downstairs.

I walked over to the window. At first I didn't see her at all. And then I caught a glimpse of something moving; she was sitting out on the swing. Alone. Alone—and waiting for someone? Was that why she went outside in the middle of the night?

Was she waiting for Saul Hogan? A. Magnuson? Clay Priestly? Dr. Somers? For Jobe?

It was a real headache, carrying my shoulder bag everywhere I went, but I didn't know what else to do. And every single time I was by myself, which was usually when I was in the bathroom, I'd read the notes over and over again.

> You were always there for me
> waiting
> but I knew you not
> You were always there
> reaching out for me
> and I did not see
> you called my name
> and I did not hear
>
> and now I see
> and now I hear
> and now I understand
> and now I love
>
> more than life itself, I love you

Was that what it felt like to be in love, really in love? And could you know someone for a long, long time and then, all of a sudden, kerplunk, fall in love?

I was so busy thinking about love that I didn't hear Mom calling me at first.

"Dodie, would you put Cissy to bed? Dad and I are going over to Annie and Frank's."

Chapter 8

Only three days until Sadie Hawkins and my date with Al Gussaro. Only ten until the last day of school. And then all summer without *having* to do anything. Loafing, playing, goofing around, no classes, no school, no assignments, no feeling guilty because I wasn't studying or writing a paper. Not that I'd been suffering much from guilt. Or from studying or writing anything. Actually, all I'd done lately was gossip with Jill, eat pies at Bruno's, daydream, and wonder about Wendy's love life. Between times, I'd read to Cissy or played Bad Guys or told her stories or played checkers.

I was just lifting some empty jelly bean packets out of our wastebasket when I saw it: pastel yellow sheets of paper. And Wendy's handwriting: *loving you.* So she was still writing notes. And tearing them up and throwing them away. Quickly I picked out all the pieces. Someone was coming up the stairs. I shoved the pieces into the pocket of my jeans and stood up. Bathroom? Too late; here was Wendy.

"What? You're not drowning yourself in the shower? Surprise," she said.

"If you don't have anything nice to say, kindly say nothing," I said. I grabbed my shoulder bag and marched out of the room, the pale yellow pieces of paper burning a hole in my pocket.

Dad was working in the darkroom. Where could I go? Bruno's? I hesitated. I could sit at one of those tables and prop my shoulder bag in front of me and put the pieces together while I was having a piece of pie.

No, not enough privacy.

Mrs. Bissell's. That was it. Holding my shoulder bag, I ran down to my bike.

I thought I'd never get there. My bike had aged a couple of generations in the last few days. Well, once the Bissells were back from California I wouldn't really need to ride it. Theirs was the only place I ever went to that wasn't walking distance.

A soft day. I propped my bike against the house and ran over to the willow tree with my shoulder bag. Perfect and private. I lay on my stomach, got out the pieces of yellow paper, and started to fit them together. I'd forgotten Scotch tape. It didn't matter, I'd tape it later.

This one was a hard one to do. All the pieces were small and pretty much the same shape. The siren blew:

was it noon? Not possibly, I'd already had lunch. I looked at my wrist. I'd left my watch at home. Anyway, it wasn't noon, unless my stomach was way off and I'd had lunch at ten.

There was enough of a breeze so the pieces of paper drifted, turned over. It took a while to get them all in order. There, finally:

> I am twice guilty
> guilty of loving you
> blindly and completely
> and of doing nothing
> to prove my love
>
> Guilty
>
> We have drugged and poisoned you
> We discuss it
> While we talk
> you lie gasping and choking
> trussed and bound
> with ribbons of cement
> while we talk, while we talk
> twice guilty are we, am I
> we sleep, we eat, we talk
> while you die, while you die

I sat and stared at the note. Then I read it again. So, it was the world that Wendy was in love with. The earth itself. Not a person, after all. Just the world.

I got all of the notes out of my shoulder bag and read them over, one by one, slowly and carefully. Not Saul Hogan, not Clay Priestly, not A. Magnuson, not Dr. Somers. And not, thank God, Jobe. It was the world that Wendy loved.

I read everything over once again, trying to put together the pieces of the puzzle, the pieces of Wendy.

She had fallen in love with the world, and she had poured all of her being into that. It was all that mattered to her, and she was angry at everything that hurt the world or threatened it. I leaned back against the tree and shut my eyes, remembering Wendy's scenes and shoutings, her tirades and her frustrated angers.

"Dodie!"

I jumped. I hadn't heard anyone coming. Now I saw a car. It was Jobe.

I felt as if I'd been caught sneaking, spying. I quickly shoved all the notes into my shoulder bag—no one must see. Waves of guilt whirled through me. What would Jobe think of me if he knew?

"Here I am," I called. I glanced on the ground around me. Had I picked up all the notes? Had any drifted away, out to the lawn? I swore I'd never pry again, never.

I ducked under the branches.

Jobe got out of the car, looking relieved. "I'll take you home, Miss Jelly Bean," he announced.

"What for? I've got my bike. How come you're here?" I couldn't get my thoughts or my words straight.

111

"Your dad wants you home."

"What's wrong?" I asked, a sudden image of Cissy, hurt, or Mom, or—

"Everyone's fine," he said hastily. "Not to worry." He smiled a smile that was deliberately reassuring.

I breathed a sigh of relief, but my heart still pounded.

"Come on," he said. "Let's get going."

"AnnTanny?" I asked suddenly.

"I told you. They're all okay. Every single one. But they want you home." He opened the car door. "Let's go."

"What's wrong?" I asked. "What's happened?"

I got in, and he backed the car around. He took a deep breath. "A big truck carrying chemicals has collided with a train, over there at the crossing at Platt's Corners. A lot of chemicals have been spilled. So everyone's got to get away. Quick."

Chemicals. I didn't even know what chemicals *were.*

"The fumes will start blowing this way. Got a hanky? May be better if you breathe through it."

"I don't have one. Just Kleenex."

"It's okay. Don't roll your window down."

"My bike," I said. My thoughts were all stuck together.

"Later."

"How did you know where I was?"

"You weren't anywhere else. Your dad called Bruno's, and you weren't there. I told him I'd track you down. I called Jill, and she said maybe you'd be over at Bissells', watering plants."

I thought of the spilled chemicals, seeping into the ground, into the body of the earth, into the lake, into the river, and I thought of the invisible poison already in the air, coming our way.

Invisible poison. I swallowed. Could I taste it?

"When we get home, what are we going to do?" I asked. We were almost there.

"Your dad will drive you all somewhere." He glanced over at me. "Don't worry. We can move a lot faster than the air, there's hardly any wind right now. But it's picking up. And there's always a chance of an explosion. It would be stupid to stay. Everyone's got to get out of town, somewhere safe."

"Somewhere safe. Where's that? How far do we have to go?"

"Not as far as the moon, at least not this time," he said. He looked at me and smiled, but the smile didn't really work. I don't know why.

"What are you going to do?" I asked.

"I'm going to get Bruno out of town. And then I'm going to get mad. Mad enough to do something. I'm going to do everything I can to keep people from poisoning and smothering and murdering this world and the creatures of this world, that's what I'm going to do. Wendy's right, you know. There's no twice. There's no

113

second chance. No second time around."

Wendy. I thought about what Jobe was saying: There's no twice.

I didn't say anything. Jobe kept talking.

"From now on, everyone's got to get mad, Dodie. Even you."

Me? What could I do?

I looked out of the closed window: other cars, other people, everyone looking blank, everyone trying to get away, trying to escape from the air.

Dad's station wagon was in the driveway. AnnTanny was sitting in the back seat, leaning back with her eyes closed. Cissy was in the seat that faced backwards, holding her dolls. Mom was just coming out of the house, carrying a big Foodster box—I could see big red letters: SOFTUNS. My blue shirt was on the top. She must be bringing extra clothes.

Dad was right behind her. "I know it's silly, but I had to bring it," he said. It was the album of pictures. It was on top of another Foodster box with clothes.

Mom called over her shoulder, "Come on, Wendy!" Uncle Frank came running around the corner with a suitcase, his glasses slipping down his nose. He got in the car beside AnnTanny and put his arm around her.

I climbed out of Jobe's car with my shoulder bag.

"I've got to be getting back," said Jobe. "Have to give Bruno a hand, get him out, too." He called to Dad, "I'll check your house on our way out and lock it up, don't worry, just go. Now."

"Let's hurry," said AnnTanny. She was pale and breathing deeply.

Jobe backed around in his car and headed down the street. I waved, but he wasn't watching.

"Wendy!" called Mom. She got into the car with the box of clothes. Everyone was pretty crowded: suitcases, boxes, paper bags, pillowcases filled with clothes and supplies.

"Let's go," said Dad. He reached inside the car and blew the horn. "Wendy!"

Buggsy. Where was Buggsy? I couldn't leave without him.

I dashed into the house. "Buggsy!" I yelled. "Buggsy!" He wasn't under the couch, he wasn't in the corner behind the big chair.

"Buggsy!"

I ran upstairs, taking two steps at a time. The horn kept honking outside.

"Buggsy!" I put my head on the floor and looked under my bed.

"You devil, Buggsy! I've looked all over for you. Why don't you ever come when I call you? Come on." I reached in and got him by the back of the neck. He started to purr.

The phone rang just as I was running downstairs. Dad

honked again. I hesitated, then grabbed the phone.

"You okay?" Jill.

"Yeah. You?"

"Sure. Jobe found you, then. He was pretty paranoid." She giggled nervously. "We're going to my grandmother's, at Rossiter. Mom said I should call, see if you all want to come with us."

"I'll ask. Everyone's jumping in the car, Dad's honking."

"So's Mom. But she wanted me to call you guys. Tell your mom it's okay if you all come to Gramma's. If there isn't room for everyone she'll find motels."

"Thanks. I'll ask. 'Bye, catch you later."

When I ran back out of the house, holding Buggsy so he couldn't possibly jump away, I saw Wendy. She was just coming around from the backyard, carrying something cupped in her hands. Cissy was still in the back of the station wagon, and I climbed in beside her. Wendy climbed in on the other side. She looked sick.

"All set?" asked Dad. We backed out of the driveway. I looked at the house and kept looking until we turned the first corner, then I could only see the porch. Then I couldn't even see it. I held Buggsy tighter.

My thoughts all jumbled around in my head. I thought about sitting under that willow tree looking out at the planted fields, and I thought about Wendy's love letters. And about Bruno's Palace and the cuckoo clock. And the sign, and the way looking outside from inside, it always said CLOSED.

The out of doors will be closed until further notice.

Suddenly I remembered Jill's call, and I told Mom, turning toward the front of the car.

"Rossiter?" asked Mom. "What do you think, John? Is it far enough?"

AnnTanny started to cough. I could see Dad looking in the rearview mirror at her.

I turned around and was facing backwards again. Wendy was staring straight ahead. Her face was streaked with dirt. What did she have in her hands? I couldn't see, Cissy was in the way.

"Dodie, can we play Bad Guys?"

I nodded. "Sure, Cissy."

"They can be monsters from outer space," she said. "And we're in a space ship, okay?" She held Lolamay Parsley and Quimby Lee tighter. "They're after us, they're after us!" she sang.

I looked over my shoulder again: Dad and Mom in the front seat, Frank and AnnTanny in the backseat, Wendy and Cissy and I facing backwards. So we could see where we'd been but not where we were going.

AnnTanny held her hands on her stomach and leaned against Frank. "How long will it be before we get where we're going?" she asked. "How many miles?"

"I can't remember whether I unplugged the coffee,"

said Mom. "Does anyone remember whether I un-plugged the coffee? Should we go back and see?"

"I unplugged it," said Dad. "I'm sure I did. Anyway, Jobe will be checking the house. Don't worry."

"Hurry," urged Cissy, nudging me. She laughed and hugged her dolls and I hugged her. The invisible Bad Guys were coming.

"I should have called the folks," said Dad. "They'll hear about it, and they'll worry. I should have called them."

"We'll call when we get there," said Mom.

Get where?

"I think I'm going to be sick," said AnnTanny. "Can we pull off the road a minute?"

"Are you sure?" asked Uncle Frank. "John, Annie's going to be sick. Can we pull off?"

"Not here," Dad said. "Up a ways."

"They're getting closer, Dodie!" whispered Cissy with delight. Wendy bowed her head over her cupped hands. No wonder her face was dirty. She was holding a clump of soil. As I looked at her she seemed to grow smaller, somehow, huddled over the little chunk of her garden, the little piece of her world. She did look like a witch, in a way, her thin face streaked, dark patches under her eyes, her body hunched over like an old woman's.

"Faster, faster," sang Cissy. "They're going to get us!" I kept looking over at Wendy, rocking back and forth. When Cissy stopped giggling, I could hear the words that Wendy was repeating over and over under her breath: "I love you, I love you, I'm sorry." Tears were running down her face into her mouth, down her chin.

Cissy sighed happily. "We're going to beat the Bad Guys again, Dodie."

"Sure we are," I said.

We were all safe, and all together. I'd be having my first date this weekend, if we got back, and school was nearly over.

And I'd found Buggsy, so everything was going to be all right.

Wasn't it?